EAM

SEVEN FACES

SEVEN FACES

Max Brand

Chivers Press
Bath, England
•
G.K. Hall & Co.
Thorndike, Maine USA

This Large Print edition is published by Chivers Press, England, and by G.K. Hall & Co., USA.

Published in 1999 in the U.K. by arrangement with Golden West Literary Agency.

Published in 1999 in the U.S. by arrangement with Golden West Literary Agency.

U.K. Hardcover ISBN 0–7540–3551–4 (Chivers Large Print)
U.K. Softcover   ISBN 0–7540–3552–2 (Camden Large Print)
U.S. Softcover   ISBN 0–7838–0360–5 (Nightingale Series Edition)

The text of this Large Print edition is unabridged.
Other aspects of the book may vary from the original edition.

Set in 16 pt. New Times Roman.

Printed in Great Britain on acid-free paper.

British Library Cataloguing in Publication Data available

Library of Congress Cataloging-in-Publication Data

Brand, Max, 1892–1944.
    Seven faces / Max Brand.
        p.   cm.
    ISBN 0–7838–0360–5 (lg. print : sc : alk. paper)
    1. Railroads—Trains—Fiction. 2. Missing persons—Fiction.
    3. Large type books. I. Title.
    [PS3511.A87S35   1999]
    813'.52—dc21   98–33782

CONTENTS

CHAPTER ONE

Last Will and Testament

Inspector Henry Corrigan of the New York Police Department missed his lunch and was late for dinner. Inspectors are expected to take such things in their stride. It is supposed that when a man rises to such a high place, he will be nourished by glory. The inspector did not feel nourished, and for hours the frown had been cutting deeper and deeper between his eyes until its blackness entered his brain. So, when the telephone call came in, he snatched up the instrument and snarled into it. His voice smoothed out when he heard the name.

'All right. Put him on,' he said. And then: 'Hello, Mister Cobb. What's the matter? Have you had another letter? I tell you what, Mister Cobb, people who write letters are usually too yellow to be dangerous. Speak up, man. The telephone isn't going to shoot you, and there's nobody listening in ... Why to Chicago? Will Chicago be any safer for you than New York? What you ought to do is to come into town and put up in some big hotel. You need to have lights and people around you. How can you *know* that you'll be murdered tonight...? Damned nonsense, Mister Cobb. I can't do it. The city of New York can't assign bodyguards to travelers. Wait a moment . . .! Two of my men are going to Chicago on a bit of work, and they may as well go now. Yes, yes, yes, Mister Cobb. The two of them together make the best man in the department. If you're going to take the late train to Chicago, they'll meet you at the gate. What will you wear? Mister Cobb, I can't guarantee anything except that Campbell and O'Rourke together will do a great many things that no other man would think of. Good bye.'

A moment later the inspector was ringing Detective Angus Campbell, saying: 'You start for Chicago on the ten thirty-five. You have to give testimony on that Rand-Weston case, and you might as well do it now . . . Yes, O'Rourke will go along with you. Get in touch with him at once. There will be a man to meet at the station, at the gate to the train. His name is John Cobb. He'll be wearing a black overcoat and a black hat. Medium height, sallow face, short, black mustache. Rather thin fellow. The fool has an idea that someone is going to murder him tonight, and he's running all the way to Chicago. Keep an eye on him. I don't care what *you* want, Campbell . . . I'm telling you that you *have* to go with O'Rourke. Come here to the office on your way to the train and get a note from me introducing you two to John Cobb. Good bye.'

The inspector, not a man given to making foolish statements, was nevertheless wrong

2

when he asserted that no one had listened in on his conversation with Cobb for, at this moment, the officer at the switchboard on the lower floor of the building was speaking softly into the big receiver which was strapped around his chest and projected in front of his face: 'Hello! That you? John Cobb is on the run. Taking the ten thirty-five for Chicago. Two detectives are going along on the same train with the inspector's orders to keep a close eye on him. One is Patrick O'Rourke. American Irish. Fat and red-faced. Always chewing a cigar, when he isn't smoking one. Looks good natured. You'll spot him easily. The other is Angus Campbell. Scotch as you find 'em. Thin, shoulders a little stooped. Sour looking. That's it. I don't know just what your game is, madame, but you'd better keep your hands off when O'Rourke and Campbell are around. Separate they're not much but, when they're together, they hate each other so much that they grind one another sharp as razors. That's all I can say, except that John Cobb will be wearing a black hat and a black coat. Good bye.'

*   *   *

The crowd entering the Grand Central at the corner of Vanderbilt Avenue and Forty-Second was thickly compacted, weighted with luggage, but Charles Latimer went through the mass like a bull moose overstepping shrubbery. He had about him the bulk of a tackle and the light step of a half-back. The loose tweeds were no more than a brownish mist over Latimer's strength, and the heavy brogans could not weight his feet. Men looked twice when they saw Latimer's back, the coat creasing a bit between the shoulder blades. Women looked twice when they saw his face. Only a sea wind, one felt, could have blown the brown so deep beneath the skin. He was a smiling fellow, not handsome but good to look at. Only when the smile stopped, something about him changed. Wood is kind to the touch; steel is grim stuff to handle. When Latimer stopped smiling, the sympathy went out of his face and left one aware of cold eyes and the broad, stubborn strength of his jaw. People who saw him on a gay evening hardly could recognize him as the same man the next morning.

When he came down the steps into the marble shimmer of the great room, under that wide dome with its curve as effortless as the sweep of the sky, he moved more slowly. For the man in the black hat and the black overcoat was being joined by two fellows near the information stand. He spoke to them with jerky nods of the head and went on with his coat collar high about his face, and his hat still pulled low. The pair, one fat and comfortable and one with the uneasy leanness of a hunting hound, fell a step behind the other and seemed to exchange glances before they proceeded briskly after him. Latimer followed them with his eyes as far as the gate of the Chicago train, then he went to the ticket window.

A girl came hurrying into the waiting line just ahead of him. Her porter stood with folded arms nearby, resting in every line. The girl herself was too pretty to be true. Too pretty to be good, was Latimer's inward phrasing, for he felt that the Creator would not lavish on a wife and mother such excess care in modeling. Eyes, for instance, are surely made to see with not merely to be seen. She was accustomed as a moving picture star or a stage favorite to the admiration of men, so that when she turned a little and found his eyes on her, her own glance blanked him out of the picture and moved calmly away.

Latimer stopped smiling and grinned.

*   *   *

Penn Station is dreary, grand, and gray. Gay wall painting cannot relieve its gloom, and all the clustering lights cannot lift its mood above that of London in the smoky murk of a fog. But Grand Central is bright, confused, charming. And everyone who takes a train from it seems bound for a happy destination. The big, resonant spaces absorb voices. Even an Englishman will speak out loud in Grand

Central Station because the noise filters away as though into the dreaminess of a summer's day. The two detectives who walked half a pace behind the man in the black coat did not utter a word either to him or to each other. Patrick O'Rourke, with a cigar fuming under the red whiskey veins of his nose, kept his hands in his overcoat pockets and stared straight before him. Skinny Angus Campbell, to whom the fumes of the cheap cigar were wafting, turned an eye as bright and cold as winter towards his companion. The porter who carried the luggage of the man in black staggered, with sagging knees, in the rear. He had heavy suitcases in each hand and smaller valises under the pressure of his elbows. It was a mule load of clumsy weight, but no one pitied him as he struggled forward, trying to go swiftly in an effort to finish his agony sooner.

The man in black stopped short, hunching his coat up around his shoulders. 'That's the car,' he said. 'I've got the drawing room in there. One of you go on ahead, please.'

'And look for what, Mister Cobb?' asked Campbell. 'Rattlesnakes, or men with machine guns?'

'For goodness sake, one of you go first!' Cobb repeated.

'All right,' said Campbell and walked into the car.

Patrick O'Rourke came a little closer to Cobb. As he spoke, he kept the cigar in the corner of his mouth, the fat of his lips stretching to accommodate speech, and the stench of the cigar fuming out in puffs toward Cobb.

'Mister Cobb,' he said, 'if you wanta get everybody looking at you, just keep that hat pulled down over your eyes and the coat hoisted up around your ears. Anybody could see that you're either sick or scared that somebody will see you.'

'Sick! That's the thing I want to look,' said Cobb. 'If they see my face . . .!'

'If who sees your face?' asked O'Rourke.

'They. They,' muttered Cobb vaguely. He fell into a coughing fit and then went on angrily, his husky voice subdued by a wheeze in his throat: 'If I knew who *they* were, wouldn't I have set the police on them? Sick. It's got to seem that I'm sick.'

Here he took O'Rourke's arm and leaned on it.

'My soul, man,' protested Cobb, choking and coughing again, 'when you smoke cigars, can't you buy the ones that are made of tobacco?'

O'Rourke endured the insult with the calm of a fat man and puffed contentedly. 'Cigars are like life,' he observed. 'What you get used to is what you want. What the hell is scaring you so much anyway, Mister Cobb?'

'They're going to murder me!' cried Cobb. 'I'll be a dead man before morning, O'Rourke.

7

Don't stand there like a senseless lump of fat. Look at the last letter.'

He dragged from his pocket a small square of brown paper on which were a few typed words:

> I'm coming for you the night of the fifteenth or before sunrise of the sixteenth, Cobb. Make your soul ready.

O'Rourke handed the paper to Campbell, who had just returned from the car. Campbell gave it a glance, snorted through his thin, pinched nose, and gave it back to Cobb.

'How is it inside?' asked Cobb anxiously, putting out a gloved hand towards Campbell.

'Why, they might all be murderers,' said Campbell. 'They got the look. I never seen anybody getting ready for bed that didn't look like a murderer. Take the collar and tie off any man and he looks ready to slog somebody on the head or stick a knife in the back.'

Cobb groaned and lifted his hand to his face, rubbing nervously at a tuft of black mustache.

'Shall we go in?' he asked.

An astonishingly pretty girl went by with the flowing step of a dancer. Her porter followed, two bags battering around his knees.

'Who's that?' demanded Cobb in a whisper. 'I've seen her somewhere. Who is she?'

'Likely from Hollywood,' said O'Rourke,

'and a first name something like Sylvia, or Rose, or Myrtle. She looks like one of the ones, all right.'

A big man in brownish tweeds, making the solid burden of a pigskin suitcase light in his left hand, went by with a quiet side glance that took in the group of three. He continued making his way down the platform.

'Why did he look at me?' asked Cobb. 'Who is that?'

'That's Timberline Bill from the Rockies,' said O'Rourke. 'He eats a fried Mexican three times a week for his liver. How in hell do I know everybody in the Grand Central?'

'He looked at me,' whispered Cobb.

'Sure he looked at you,' answered O'Rourke. 'Everybody's gonna look at you and wonder where you got the chills and fever.'

'True. True. What am I doing to stand out here? Get me inside. Get me inside.'

O'Rourke walked first, this time, waddling down the aisle of the sleeper through a barrage of black looks from people who were standing at their bunks arranging matters inside and getting ready to enclose themselves for a night of joltings and sudden stoppages, nightmares and frightened wakings. All strangers are enemies, particularly in a sleeping car. In the wake which O'Rourke left behind him, Cobb went down the length of the car to the drawing room, Number A. Campbell followed. When they were inside, Cobb shrank back into the

9

narrow corner near the door.

'The window-curtain!' he gasped. 'The light!'

Campbell pulled down the curtain. O'Rourke switched out the lights except one small, red globe, and Cobb groaned with relief. This dim light left all faces compositions of tarry black shadows and wavering features. The eyes, in particular, were deep pools of darkness that held one uncertain, luminous point.

'You like it all graveyard like this?' asked O'Rourke.

'They can't see in, now,' said Cobb.

'They won't need to,' answered O'Rourke, 'you'll scare yourself to death before morning. Listen, Mister Cobb, why didn't you go and get police protection at your home? A bird that starts running away is the one that gets shot at.'

'Protection at home?' said Cobb in the same husky voice. 'The men sent to guard me might be the ones hired by him to murder me!'

'If you look at it that way,' said O'Rourke, 'maybe Campbell and me have been bought up, too. Maybe we're the ones that are gonna blow you down.'

Cobb shrank smaller in the corner of the seat and said nothing. He turned his head quickly, like the swiftly pivoting head of a bird, to look first at O'Rourke and then at Campbell.

'Ah, shut up your nonsense, O'Rourke,' said Campbell. 'You waste everybody's time with

10

your gabble. I'd rather listen to a guinea-hen cackle.'

Cobb drew a breath of relief and settled back in the seat again. A moment later he had dropped his face between his two gloved hands. Without audible warning, without the slightest jarring, the great train began to roll over the rails as smoothly as water down an endless flume. It gathered speed. Cobb lifted his head from his hands.

'You forgot something?' asked O'Rourke.

Cobb, without answering, pulled an envelope from his pocket and took out a fountain pen. He began to write with painful slowness, pausing when a lurch of the train disturbed his hand. The light was so dim that he had to bend far over to study the paper which he held on his bony knee.

'Have a flash of light now, brother?' asked O'Rourke.

'No, no. No!' cried Cobb.

'Rabbits are like that ... and cats,' said O'Rourke. 'They like the dark. It makes the rabbits feel safer, and the cats do their best hunting then.'

'You have to talk. That's all. You have to talk!' exclaimed Campbell. 'Here. I'll hold a flashlight for you, Mister Cobb.'

'A flashlight,' said Cobb. 'Well ... yes ... thank you, Campbell.'

Campbell snapped out a small pocket torch that threw a core of white light on the envelope and paler outer margins over the trousers of Cobb. He had not taken off his gloves, so great was his eagerness to put down his idea at once.

Campbell read without great difficulty, in spite of the continual waverings which the motion of the train caused:

> I, John Cobb, being in my right mind and in full possession of my senses, though in fear of death before the morning, do hereby give and bequeath to my beloved cousin, Lawrence Purvis Pelton, as my sole heir, all my property in real estate, cash, or otherwise, of whatever nature.
>
> (Signed)   *John Cobb*
> (Witnessed) ....
>   ....

The jerking, uncertain writing grew suddenly more smoothly fluent as the familiar flow of the signature came off the pen.

'Will you read this and witness it?' asked Cobb.

Campbell grunted: 'You know what you're doing, man? You're rich. Are you gonna pour all that you've got into one hopper?'

'Will you sign? Will you sign?' demanded Cobb impatiently.

'Well . . .' muttered Campbell, shaking his Scotch head.

Cobb groaned.

He signed forthwith, and Cobb snatched pen and envelope to offer both to O'Rourke.

The Irishman signed without more to do but, as he handed back the document to Cobb, he said calmly: 'Well, you're *worth* murdering now . . . to Lawrence Purvis Pelton.'

'Pelton?' said Cobb, angrily. 'He's in the West. I telephoned to him this morning.'

'Ay,' said O'Rourke, 'but maybe he ain't too poor to hire some helping hands, brother!'

CHAPTER TWO

Telegram for Miss Worth

The unpleasant suggestion which O'Rourke had made did not weigh very long upon the nervous spirit of Mr. Cobb. He shrank back into his corner for a moment so that, between the turned-up velvet collar of his coat and the turned-down brim of his hat, his face was a mere smudge of darkness. Then he rallied and sat up straight. He held out the signed and witnessed envelope with a stiff, straight arm, like that of a fencer, to Campbell.

'I want you to take this,' he ordered crisply. 'Murder . . . they can't rub out this will. They can't steal the future of my property. What does a man live by? By his assets.'

As Campbell took the envelope, frowning,

Cobb gripped both hands together hard and broke into two or three notes of high-pitched laughter. There was something so strange about the key and the sound of his laughter that O'Rourke, who was as keenly sensitive to sounds as he was indifferent to smells, started a little and looked again at Cobb.

Cobb said shortly: 'Well, that's that. I don't need you now. Not for a while. Every half hour, one of you come and knock at this door. If it's not opened by me, have the porter open it . . . have him break it down . . . smash it down and get in.'

His voice had gone up almost to a scream. He got to his feet with a hand clutching the breast of his overcoat.

'Aw, steady, steady!' said O'Rourke. 'You got a lot of life in you yet. Buck up, brother. Why shouldn't any of us stay right in here with you?'

'I want to be alone. I have to be alone,' said Cobb. 'Stay here with one of you . . .? Go to sleep with eyes watching me? My God, I couldn't stand it! No, no. Get out. Please. Every half hour, come back. Just knock and look in.'

'You mean,' said O'Rourke, 'that we're gonna stay awake all night and take a look at you every half hour?'

'Why not? Why not?' shrilled Cobb. 'Ah, wait a moment! I understand. I didn't mean for nothing. Here, take this. And you. I didn't

14

mean for nothing. For goodness' sake, my friends, keep a close watch. Observe every face on the train. Mark down every suspicious person.'

He pushed a bill into O'Rourke's hand and another into Campbell's.

O'Rourke crumpled the paper as though it were for the wastepaper basket before he shoved it into a trousers pocket with a forefinger. He said: 'You want one of us to stand outside the door of the stateroom?'

'And mark the place where I'm located on this train? Am I insane? Have I lost my wits, or did you ever have any?' screamed Cobb. 'So that at the first stop the murderers could bomb this end of the car? Have you no sense at all, O'Rourke?'

The two detectives left the stateroom. They went on back to the lounge car, where Campbell took a look at his watch.

'Half hour. I'll take the first turn,' he said.

O'Rourke said: 'How much you get?'

'Fifty dollars,' said Campbell, and a smile twitched one side of his mouth.

'Yeah? Look!' growled O'Rourke.

He was gathering a fresh cigar into the loose of his lips with a singular dexterity, biting off the end, and ejecting the fragment from the corner of his mouth without supporting the cigar for a moment with his hand. The prehensile capacity of both upper and lower lips made this unnecessary. He flicked on the

15

flame of his lighter and smiled down at it as he started his cloud of smoke. Campbell studied the bill and handed it back.

'A century, eh?' he said.

'A hundred smacks,' O'Rourke agreed, pocketing the money with his former nonchalance. 'How much has this bird John Cobb got all together?'

'Fifteen millions,' said Campbell, slowly sinking into a chair beside that of O'Rourke, his eyes lost in a trance of thought. 'Divide that by three for the facts. Five millions.'

'A guy can't pile up that much from nothing without having a brain,' said O'Rourke. 'A guy can't make that much without being a judge of men.'

'Meaning that he picked you out for the hundred and me for the fifty?' asked Campbell.

'Meaning? I wasn't meaning nothing,' protested O'Rourke with elaborate carelessness, shrugging his shoulders and looking away for a moment.

Campbell licked the pallor of his thin lips and stared fixedly at O'Rourke. He said not a word.

'This cluck of a John Cobb,' O'Rourke went on. 'What do you think? Just cuckoo, or a plain fool?'

'A man who makes fifteen millions has to have a brain,' Campbell echoed.

'Maybe,' agreed O'Rourke. 'There ain't

fifteen million dollars' worth of luck in the world. How did Cobb make his money?'

'You got assigned to this job, didn't you?' Campbell snarled. 'Why don't you look up the facts for yourself? Cobb made his stake out West. He was hitched to some phony mining deals. Then the gold price went up, and he sold out for his big stake. Why don't you work up your own stuff?'

'I keep my time for the big things,' O'Rourke rumbled, with his grin spilling from his cigar far across the other side of his face. 'I don't do the secretary work.'

Campbell swallowed. He said pleasantly: 'Maybe that's why they assign me such a lot to the same cases with you . . . so's I can do the secretary job?'

'Maybe. I been wondering,' said O'Rourke.

The thin hand of Campbell opened like a pair of jaws, seized a portion of the thin air, and strangled it with a slow compression of the fingers.

'I been wondering too,' said Campbell, nodding. 'I thought perhaps it was because they didn't want to turn a soggy Irish drunk loose by himself.'

'Never drunk, boy,' O'Rourke corrected, resting a hand momentarily on Campbell's shoulder with an air of beneficent kindness. 'The Irish never get drunk. Only good natured.'

A purple spot appeared on Campbell's

17

cheek.

'Take your hand off my shoulder!' he murmured.

'Sure,' said O'Rourke, letting the hand slowly slide away. 'Friendship is the sort of thing that a Scotchman never could understand.'

A uniformed lad came into the lounge car, saying rapidly, softly: 'Miss Worth? Miss Worth? Miss Josephine Worth? Telegram for you, Miss Worth.'

He had stopped halfway down the car where that amazingly pretty girl was sitting. She put down her magazine and, looking up to take the message, showed the slight smile of beauty, not of consciousness, that stayed on her lips.

'She holds her eyes right straightforward, like she was in a spotlight,' said O'Rourke. 'I dunno where she's going, but it costs more'n four cents a mile.'

'Rotten,' said Campbell. 'You're always rotten. I've seen pigs that would rather eat spoiled apples than fresh ones.'

'Listen,' said O'Rourke, 'why don't you sit someplace else? I've got all the information that I want out of you. Every time I look at you, it reminds me when I was a poor little boy, and the winter mornings were getting into my chilblains. Get the hell out, will you?'

Campbell started to rise in a rage. Then he settled back. He was hunting rapidly for words, his eyes blinking, but he could find nothing to say.

'Here, steward,' said O'Rourke. 'Couple Scotch highballs, will you? Kind of on the run, brother, eh?'

The waiter went out with his white apron swishing. Now as Miss Josephine Worth sat with bowed head, her fur boa slipped from her lap to the floor and, as she leaned to pick it up, a big, brown hand forestalled her. She looked up at the huge form of the man.

'My name is Latimer, Miss Worth,' he said. 'Don't creep back to your compartment and sit there and shiver with your bad news. Take your chair again and have a drink with me. You need a drink. You're sick. Settle back and tip down your head a little. Then nobody will see how sick you are, and how white. If you walk back through the train, looking like this, everybody'll know that hell is to pay.'

She looked at the brown of his face and his smile, which seemed an earnest of helpfulness. Then she slipped back into her chair.

'Cognac,' said Latimer to the waiter. 'Two. That *Courvoisier*. The old stuff.'

Up the aisle, O'Rourke was passing a glass.

'This'll do you good,' he was saying to Campbell.

Campbell had the glass almost to his lips when he remembered with a start.

'Drink with you? I'd rather drink with swine out of a trough!'

He put the glass back with a jar that started

19

the liquid sloshing from side to side. O'Rourke was merely laughing. Campbell snatched a paper and pretended to read.

'I can blot 'em both up, brother,' chortled O'Rourke. 'My gosh, how it must be burning you up to miss a free drink!'

Campbell looked at his watch. The half hour was up, and he went hastily down the aisle. Behind him he could feel, rather than hear, the pulsation of O'Rourke's laughter. He could see in his mind's eye the large, loose face spilled into hearty mirth.

CHAPTER THREE

Meeting in the Night

In the lounge car sat a man strikingly foreign in appearance. He wore a short, pointed, black beard, and his heavy, black eyebrows were arched with an odd openness of expression. His black hair flowed long and thick. He had no mustaches to go with the beard, and this left clear to view the red of his full lips, a young mouth in the midst of that middle-aged face. He might have been a stage villain, or a German from the Rhine, or a Frenchman of an old school. The flow of his big, soft tie somehow gave assurance that he was first of all a fraud.

20

Perhaps he had Southern ancestors and wished to dress the part, using 1860 as his model. At any rate, in his heart Aloysius Grosvenor was a confidence man, though he could not have won the ear of anyone except a child or an old woman, he had put so much false gentility on his back. To look at him was to think of Bowie knives and lynchings and mint juleps and shadowy verandahs.

Aloysius Grosvenor now rose from his chair and stood for a moment to pull down his waistcoat a little and straighten his coat. He liked to make these pauses whenever he rose to his full height, so that anyone who wished would be able to look their fill upon him. Then he walked with slow dignity down the aisle, and it seemed to him that the ladies, as he went by, were turning their heads and gazing with covert admiration after him. For females he felt a generous compassion not untinged with contempt.

He went straight back through the train and stood for a moment outside the door of the stateroom which O'Rourke and Campbell were guarding. Someone was snoring in an upper berth nearby. Here and there were bulges in the heavy green curtains, where a sleeper lay crookedly in his bed. When Grosvenor had surveyed this scene with his usual calm, he rapped on the stateroom door. He had to repeat the knock before the door swung half open.

21

'Well? Well?' snapped a quick, nervous voice.

'It's just old Al,' said Grosvenor. 'Old Al Grosvenor.'

He put out his big foot. The door jarred heavily against the sole of it. The steel door creaked a little.

'Don't be that way,' said Grosvenor. 'You want to see me, don't you?'

The door opened again, a faltering, hesitant motion.

'Yes, Al. Of course I want to. Come in.'

'If you want to see me, switch on the light so you can have a chance,' chuckled Grosvenor.

'Well, hurry in!' bade the other.

The lights clicked on. The smaller man stood blinking at that startling brightness as Grosvenor strode in and pushed the door shut behind him. He put the weight of his broad shoulders against the wall and towered over his host as he stated: 'I've got a gun. If you make any funny moves, I'll smash your skull in with the butt of it, you rat-faced son of Belial.'

The other looked up at Grosvenor, not with fear but with a steady, cold, poisonous hate in his eyes. He shrank from the narrow passage at the door and took the place where he had been sitting before. His body seemed to shrink smaller in his clothes. His face was white but again, it seemed, not with fear so much as with overwhelming horror and disgust. He kept watching Grosvenor as one might watch a dangerous beast that has escaped from behind bars.

Grosvenor, taking the opposite place, pulled out a cigar, bit off the end, spat it upon the floor, and lighted his smoke. All the while he continued his survey of the other, brightly attentive, pleased with himself, but extremely upon the *qui vive* for things sudden and unexpected. As he smoked, his lips grew moist and shone a brighter red than ever, as though he had been eating something syrupy and sweet and had neglected wiping his mouth.

'Glad, aren't you?' asked Grosvenor.

For an answer, he had silence and those drifting, watchful eyes.

Grosvenor laughed. 'You know how I feel?' he asked. 'I feel like I'd sat down facing one of those damned little side-winding rattlesnakes that're apt to jump and bite you in the face. I can feel your eyes take hold of me like that.'

He took a pinch out of the air with thumb and forefinger. His nails were manicured with the care an anxious girl might give to her hands. His fingers really were slender, tapering, beautiful. Usually he kept them encased in gloves and, even now as he smoked, his left hand was still gloved.

'Are you going to talk, or sit there and blink?' asked Grosvenor.

'I'll talk.'

'Kind of a health trip you're taking?'

'No.'

23

'Go right ahead and spill the beans,' said Grosvenor. 'I dunno, but I guess that I've got you where I always wanted to have you.'

'You have.'

'Oh, you're gonna admit it, are you?' asked Grosvenor, suddenly so interested that he leaned forward and rested his left elbow on his knee.

'I admit it.'

'You look sick.'

'I feel sick.'

'It does me a lot of good to see you like this,' declared Grosvenor. 'Outside of having you down and stamping your face off, I can't think of anything that I'd rather see than the whites of your eyes when you roll 'em like that. How scared are you?'

'I'm not scared. I'm sick.'

Grosvenor drew in a long, long breath and shook his head.

'You are. By Harry, you are,' he said. 'You're sick. What kind of poison's killing you?'

'I've got to talk. Just give me a little time. I need to get my breath.'

'Yeah, and arrange the lies you'll tell.'

Grosvenor, watching, saw a strange smile twitch at the corners of the other's mouth.

Then the odd answer came: 'No, Al. I can't lie. It's the first time in my life that I can't lie. There's nothing I can do. I'm trapped. The moment I saw you, I knew I was trapped. I tried to slam the door in your face, and it seemed to me that it was the teeth of the trap closing over me, sinking into my soul.'

'Soul?' said Grosvenor. He laughed a little, keeping his delighted eyes upon the other. 'There ain't a thing you can do, eh?'

'There's nothing. Literally nothing. If I had the brains of an angel, still there would be nothing to do.'

'You've got to sit and take it, eh?' asked Grosvenor.

'That's what I've got to do.'

'Don't it damn' near kill you to have your hands strapped behind you?' asked Grosvenor.

'That's what it does. It just about kills me. I feel as though I were dying now.'

'You look it, too,' gloated Grosvenor.

'Well, I'll have to make my start.'

'Take your time,' said Grosvenor. 'Plan the way you're going to deal your cards.'

'Face up.'

'The hell you will,' drawled Grosvenor. 'You couldn't make a straight deal. Not if you were on the edge of hell.'

He watched the singular smile that rewarded this remark and listened with starting eyes as he heard the answer:

'I'm not on the edge of hell. I'm *in* hell. I'm in the center of it.'

'In hell and in my hands,' said Grosvenor. 'I guess that's about the same thing.'

'Not entirely, but almost.'

25

'Start in with the yarn, then.'

'Steady yourself, Grosvenor.'

'Words can't do anything to me,' answered Grosvenor. 'I've absorbed too much lead in my day . . . words don't matter.'

'What's the biggest stake you've ever had?'

'About a quarter of a million.'

'Divide by five. Perhaps you've had fifty thousand at your peak, eh?'

Grosvenor shrugged his shoulders. He even laughed. 'All right,' he said. 'Call it anything you want. You always were a damned kind of smart snake at that.'

'Now listen to me. You're going to be rich.'

'That's good news. How rich?'

'About ten million dollars.'

'Ah, my golly,' said Grosvenor, whispering.

'Don't let your cigar go out. I said ten millions. I'd rather see the money go to a baboon. That's what you are. A brainless ape. You're a face . . . you're not a man. You're a great, fat, roosting swine. You've only got an instinct to do wrong, and you haven't the wit to raise the devil that you'd like to. But . . . you're to get ten million dollars!'

Grosvenor had changed color. His mouth sagged, but his widened eyes were busy drinking in the enormous hope.

'Ten millions,' he whispered, and the sudden outthrust of his jaw told that he felt the money was his, that he would keep, defend that huge fortune. It was as though he had

26

acquired it by right.

'It comes to you because you happened to be here on this train. Tell me something, Grosvenor. You just happened to be here?'

'Put it that way. Now go on.'

'I'll go on,' said a voice that groaned as it uttered the words.

'And all the cards face up, mind you,' said Grosvenor.

'Damn you and what you want! It's what I have to give. That's what kills me.'

He closed his eyes and held out both hands to keep the thought away from him. Afterwards he made a great effort and mastered himself. He began to speak in a hard, steady, monotonous voice, and the sweat formed on the face of Grosvenor as he listened. It gathered in beads that ran together and started small rivulets that ran down his face to the thick of his beard.

CHAPTER FOUR

Locked Door

In the lounge car, when the cognac came, the girl lifted her glass and tried to smile at Latimer. It was like turning a light on and off; the darkness seemed thicker. Without the smile, which was her gift from heaven, she was shrewdly altered, stripped to a strange nakedness, and grown younger until she seemed hardly more than a child. She held the glass a moment at her lips before she drank a sip and then a small swallow. Her head inclined as she put down the glass.

'How is it?' asked Latimer.

'It's good, thank you,' said Josephine Worth.

'You been a lot in France?' he asked.

She looked up suddenly at him. He could not say that color was back in her face, but it was less startlingly white. Trouble was still in her eyes, but it was being strongly repressed. Thought was there beside it.

As she began to speak, the slight smile returned to her lips.

'You know that I've a compartment. You know that I've been to France. What else, Mister Latimer?' she asked.

After she had spoken, he continued to enjoy her for a moment before he answered half absently: 'Chicago was as good for me as where I was going. After I bought a ticket to your place, I thought I might as well look up your address on the train. Do you mind?'

All the trouble left her eyes, and only the thought remained in them. 'I don't mind at all,' she said, studying him.

'About France . . . you wanted that drink. You needed it. But you had to stop to try the bouquet of it an instant before you tried it and then took a swallow. On this side of the water

28

we don't ask questions with our noses. We just gulp and wait for the effect.'

She leaned back in the chair and let her head rest against the cushion. It did not matter who saw her now, for the color was almost entirely restored.

She said: 'If you want to talk, please do . . . I like to hear you.'

'I've got a nice straight left and a one-two punch,' said Latimer. 'Can you use them on your troubles?'

She looked out the opposite windows, where the bright image of the car swayed and trembled behind the glimmer of the glass. Through the image trailed vague masses, trees, houses, and lights smeared out into lines by the speed of the train.

'I can't use them,' she said.

She drew off her gloves to lift the cognac glass again. Her hands were a good 20th-Century brown.

'Where did you buy that tan? Florida?' he asked.

'Ultra violet,' she said, turning her head part of the way and her eyes the rest.

'Do you have to be as careful as that?'

'Yes.' She looked at him steadily. The smile would not leave her, but he saw the gravity in her eyes. 'I don't dare to spoil the picture.'

'Josephine Worth only has a pretty face and about twenty-five hundred bucks,' suggested Latimer. He listened to the brutality of his own remark and added to it: 'So she has to make time and cut corners.'

'Josephine has a hundred and twenty-five dollars and a Hollywood trousseau,' she said, impervious to his bluntness. She added to her sentence, as he had done to his: 'But she doesn't cut corners.'

'I thought it was something like Hollywood,' he said.

'Everyone does. That's the trouble.'

'The more the better,' said Latimer.

'Don't you see?' said the girl, and she made a quick gesture that almost touched her face, modeling the line of it. 'There's not enough character in the features. Not nearly enough.'

'Too perfect,' said Latimer, nodding. 'No fly in the ointment. Too good to be true.'

Here he found her looking at him again, weighing him calmly and accurately. 'This sort of stuff is only right for the chorus,' she said.

She threw the idea of 'such stuff' away with an open-handed gesture.

'I saw something was wrong, and that was why I decided to come along,' smiled Latimer.

'Do you like to say things like that,' she asked, 'because you think people will believe them, or because you know that they won't?'

'When a fellow weighs more than two hundred pounds,' said Latimer, 'he has to be silly. A big man who's also serious is a lot too much to be taken in single doses.'

'Is that why?' said the girl. She looked out

the windows again. Heavy rain was beginning to slant strokes of wet across them. The image of the interior was a spotted haze, and the lights outside blurred together with startled scatterings of rays. The smile of the girl deepened as she shook her head. She laughed a little.

'Don't worry me like this, please,' said Latimer.

'You're not like the rest,' she answered. 'You have reasons and everything.'

Here she surprised him with a sidelong glance and found that his face for the first time was entirely sober. It was hard brown rock, and the eyes made her wince a little. This expression passed from him almost instantly and left him smiling.

'I'll be back in a few minutes,' he said, rising.

He went down the aisle with his big, easy stride. The train hit a curve and groaned to it with a deep side-sway, but Latimer went on with a perfect balance.

The girl, looking after him, waited until he had passed from view at the end of the car. Then she rose and followed him with that flowing suppleness of step which, to see, was always to remember.

'Sailor, that big bird,' said O'Rourke to Campbell.

'Sailor?' said Campbell, drawn by his thought to forgetfulness that he was not speaking to O'Rourke. 'Yeah, sailor, or

31

anything hard. He looks to me like . . .'

Here he remembered how much he was detesting O'Rourke and closed his teeth with a click. O'Rourke, all understanding, laughed his loud, brawling laughter and consulted his second drink. It was at this moment that the brakes of the train went on with an oily suddenness and brought it to a stop. There was a wait of a few moments, then it resumed its headway again.

A little later than this—about two or three minutes, they estimated afterward—O'Rourke looked at his watch and said: 'Well, my turn, I suppose.'

He got up, yawned, threw back his shoulders, and felt the pull of his belt against his stomach.

'I'm gonna take up exercise,' said O'Rourke to himself and went slowly down the aisle.

When he came to Cobb's car, he saw, through the jiggling curtains of the washroom, the colored porter asleep, with his head lying on one shoulder as though the neck were broken. The mouth of the Negro was open. The jolting of the train made his lips move as though he were whispering a secret to a ghost.

O'Rourke stepped on to the stateroom and rapped at the door of it. He waited, rapped again vainly, and then pounded heavily with the heel of his palm.

A drunken voice sounded behind him. He turned and saw a man in the adjoining upper

32

berth sticking out his head and holding a half-emptied pint flask.

'Listen,' said the drunk. 'Don't you go on bozzerin' him for drink. Bozzer me. Bozzer this pint.'

'Pull in your ears,' said O'Rourke.

The drunk looked sadly upon him and suddenly collapsed behind the curtains of his bed. O'Rourke went to the porter and shook him so that his curly head jogged up and down, back and forth.

'Stateroom A,' said O'Rourke. 'Open it for me. Open it fast.'

The porter wakened, stared at him with a sort of angry hopelessness, and then staggered before him to Stateroom A.

There he turned and demanded: 'What you want? Who wants to know?'

'I'm Detective O'Rourke from headquarters,' he said. 'Open that up!'

'My good Lord,' said the porter and fitted a key into the lock.

He turned it back and forth and began to shake his head.

'He's got it latched right home,' said the porter. 'I guess the key won't work. You knocked for him right loud?'

'I knocked for him,' said O'Rourke.

The porter lifted his foot and kicked half a dozen times. The clangor brought twenty heads out from behind curtains. Angry voices snarled up the aisle.

O'Rourke remained heedless of them, leaning his hand pensively against the door. He was seeing only the will which had been scrawled on the back of the envelope by John Cobb. Fifteen million of even newspaper dollars is a lot of money.

CHAPTER FIVE

Vanished!

The wheels roared and did their clicking catch-step over the rail junctions beneath. The powerful steel springs rocked the weight of the car with a long, trundling motion. O'Rourke, looking hazily over his shoulder, saw the big fellow in the brownish tweed coming up the aisle. O'Rourke stopped him with a raised finger.

'Try your shoulder on that door,' he asked. 'Latched on the inside.'

'What's the matter?' asked Latimer.

'Why, I dunno,' said O'Rourke. 'Murder, maybe.'

He waited until the eye of the big man settled on him and turned cold with seriousness.

'All right,' said Latimer. 'Lend me your gun, just in case.'

O'Rourke unholstered the weapon, handed

34

it over.

Latimer tried the doorknob with his hand, as though the feel of it might tell him something. Then he stepped back a pace, crouched, and drove his weight at the door. The bulging shoulder muscles cushioned the shock. The door squealed like a rat underfoot and jogged a fraction of an inch open. Latimer stepped back again.

'Football?' asked the porter.

'Yeah,' said O'Rourke absently.

Latimer struck again. The door banged open and let him go floundering into the interior. He was half lost in that red-tinged dimness, but the hand of the porter found the switch at once and snapped on the lights.

'Why, there's nobody here at all!' said Latimer, rubbing the shoulder that had absorbed those two mighty shocks. Silently he returned O'Rourke's revolver.

O'Rourke looked around him calmly. The first look is worth everything, he knew. He thought of Campbell hunched over a newspaper in the lounge car, and his lips twitched with a sort of disgusted triumph.

One window had been raised as far as it would go, and the rain, slashing in aslant, had turned a section of the red plush of the seat black with wet that trickled to the floor again, drop by drop.

'Here,' said the porter. 'Here's where that damn' fool pulled the alarm signal and stopped the train a while back. Look! Here's where it was pulled. He'll pay for that.'

'I guess he's paid for it,' said O'Rourke, inquiring of the air with distended nostrils.

He found what he wanted in the corner near the couch. It was a small bottle with not a drop of liquid left inside, but the strong reek of chloroform went up the nostrils of O'Rourke as he sniffed at the open mouth of the phial.

He looked at the luggage, counted the four pieces of it, made sure that all were strapped securely. Then he leaned out the window. Something wet and hard and rough slapped him smartly across the face. It was not the blow but the fear that made O'Rourke duck back into the stateroom with his hand on his revolver.

He saw the thing move again through the darkness beyond the window with a snaky curving. He reached out and caught the end of a rope. When he pulled, it resisted strongly. He jerked hard but the rope remained in place. It was stout, new, shining, half-inch manila.

O'Rourke turned. Half a dozen passengers in pajamas were clustered at the open door of the stateroom. He shut it in their faces.

He said to Latimer: 'You see a fellow sitting with me back there in the lounge? Scrawny kind of a half-starved bird with his head hung out forward on the end of his neck like a jack-o'-lantern on a stick? Name of Campbell. Mind going and telling him that I want him

36

here? You might say that Cobb's gone.'

Latimer nodded and left.

'What's the next town?'

'Buffalo, boss,' said the porter. 'You think that gentleman heaved himself out the window?'

'I mean the next town along this line,' answered O'Rourke.

'Bingham,' said the porter. 'But we don't . . .'

'Yes, we do,' said O'Rourke. 'Get the word forward to the engineer. We stop at Bingham. I'm O'Rourke, of the headquarters force in New York. Homicide squad. Mind that . . . homicide squad.'

'Yes, sir. Yes, boss,' said the porter, rubbing his shoulders against the wall as he tried to get distance from this terrible man of the crime world.

'Wait a moment. Where'd we stop down the line? Where'd the emergency signal stop the train?'

'Right the other side of Fullerton,' said the porter. 'I looked out for a minute and seen a couple piles of ties by the way and the lights of Fullerton sprinkled around in the night just beyond. You can tell Fullerton because it's got three lights right up top on the hill and . . .'

'Stop this train at Bingham. Get about it!' commanded O'Rourke.

Campbell came in with big Latimer behind him.

37

'What's your name, brother?' asked O'Rourke.

'Charles Latimer,' he answered.

'Thanks for helping out. Don't need you any more, Latimer. Thanks very much.'

Latimer left the stateroom. The door would not close entirely on account of the smashed lock.

'Well?' said Campbell, standing in the middle of the space between the two seats and poking out his head from side to side. 'How?'

He found the chloroform flask the next moment and sniffed at it. Then his bright little eyes waited, like two twinkling stars, on the explanation from O'Rourke, the first man on the spot.

'The way of it ain't so hard to see.'

He caught, again, the dangling rope end outside the window and shoved it to Campbell.

'This rope's anchored to the top of the car,' said O'Rourke. 'Fellow lies up there. He knows what reservation Cobb's made, and he lies out up there and waits for a good time. Then he takes his chance and walks down the rope till he's beside the window. Cobb's in here. Asleep, likely. The fellow outside works the window up . . .'

'He hangs on with one hand and works the window up, eh?' asked Campbell, sneering. 'And the train hitting up seventy through the wind, and the rope greasy with rain?'

'Works the window up,' O'Rourke went on,

38

hating Campbell quietly with his eyes, 'and then slides up the shade.'

'And Cobb still sleeps?' asked Campbell.

'The jitters he was in, he'd be asleep hard and fast as soon as the pressure was taken off him. So then the fellow eases his way in through the window. He's got the chloroform ready. He claps it over Cobb's mug in a handkerchief, say. When Cobb quits kicking, the lad pulls the alarm signal to stop the train. When it eases up, he slides Cobb through the window, drops after him, and carts him away.'

'Why?' asked Campbell.

'Why is anybody with fifteen million berries kidnapped?' asked O'Rourke. 'Be your age, Methuselah.'

'This job was done inside the train, not from the roof of it,' said Campbell.

'Go on and talk. You don't bother me with your talking,' said O'Rourke. 'You're so damned wrong that sometimes you give me the right ideas.'

'Roof of the car! How could a man lie up on the roof of a car? How did he get there? Couldn't have been there while the train was in the station, or he would have been seen. Couldn't have got up there after the train started moving,' Campbell insisted.

O'Rourke jerked on the end of the rope. 'Seeing things ain't enough for you, Angus,' he said. 'You gotta chaw and swaller them before you're sure.'

39

'I'm sure of Corrigan,' answered Campbell. 'I'm sure of the hell he'll raise when he finds out that Cobb got through our fingers.'

'Who'd have it any other way?' answered O'Rourke. 'If Cobb hadn't been grabbed, we wouldn't have anything to think about. It might have been some good guy that we'd be sorry about. But it's only a dirty, sneakin', yella dog ... that John Cobb. Leave me see the will, Angus.'

Campbell drew out the document, looked at O'Rourke through a moment of doubt, and then handed it over. O'Rourke, disregarding the writing on the back of the envelope, pulled out the fold of paper which the letter contained. He read aloud from the sharp-angled script:

Dear John:

I'm about to give up the airplane. You're right. Even with liquor out of the picture, I haven't the sort of nerves that do well in the air. I'm looking about now to try to find someone who will buy the machine, but second-hand airplanes are less welcome than poor relations.

I've read over carefully the copies of the letters which you sent along. I can't make up my mind about them. I'd like to call them a gigantic hoax, but there's a little note of grimness about them that inclines me to take them almost seriously. There *are* people who'd be glad to put a knife into you—or into me. They'd rather knife us than have money. Is it possible that some devilish freak of that sort has gotten on your trail?

My dear old fellow, take care of yourself. My advice is, first of all, to get in touch with the police and ask for protection. You know Corrigan, and if there's anything he can do for you, he ought to do it. My next advice— and think this over seriously—is that you should take a train and come straight out here to see me. To stay as long as you can. If trouble comes near us here, we can see it starting over the horizon twenty miles away! Think this over and let me know what you'll do.

Always affectionately,
Larry

O'Rourke said: 'This Larry is the Lawrence Purvis Pelton who's the "beloved cousin" of John Cobb. Maybe Pelton is fifteen million dollars richer, right now, than he was this morning.'

'If this was murder,' said Campbell, 'tell me why they had to chloroform Cobb and drag him through the window of the train?'

'I dunno,' answered O'Rourke. 'But murder has a sort of a smell about it. Murder is what I smell. Murder is what Cobb expected. Murder is what he got. Who gets off the train when she stops at Bingham up the line, here?'

'Neither of us does,' said Campbell. 'We go on to Chicago and turn in the evidence that hangs Rand and Weston. We can take this up on the backtrail.'

'You stick on the train, brother,' said O'Rourke. 'I'm getting off. Your evidence on Rand and Weston is as good as mine. About the only thing you know how to do is to talk to a jury. Maybe because talk don't cost anything. You stick on the train, and I'll go off and find Cobb for Corrigan.'

'Go and be damned,' said Campbell. 'While you're gone, I'll find the murderer by checking who's missing off the train.'

He gloated over O'Rourke through the simple effectiveness of this idea and then left the stateroom.

CHAPTER SIX

The Man in the Alcove

The train slowed for Bingham and waited there, panting for two full minutes before the checkup was completed. The conductor reported to the two detectives: 'There's not a soul missing. We've waked up everybody on the train and been damned for it. Everyone's aboard.'

42

O'Rourke turned up the collar of his overcoat before stepping down into the drive of the rain. He grinned vastly around his cigar at Campbell.

'You get the goose egg, brother,' he said.

'If nobody's left the train,' said Campbell, his eyes glittering, 'that means that the chloroformer is still on it. Go wade in the mud, O'Rourke. I'll stay here on the train and find the crook between drinks ... Have a good time. It's what you were meant for, you bog jumper!'

The calm superiority of O'Rourke was damaged by his last words. He almost dropped the cigar from his mouth as he started to shout an answer. But since the train was already beginning to move stealthily, he changed his mind and lurched from the last step down to the platform. He grabbed the suitcase which was shoved after him and then ducked his head against the whistling force of the rain.

Over him ran the lights of the train, slowly, then in a rapid blur. The last platform whisked past before he had started to walk to the little station house. By the time he reached it, the next bend had eaten up the long line of the sleepers and the brightness of the lounge car at the end of the train.

The station house was empty, dark, blind. O'Rourke stood in the lee of it, listening to the crash of the rain and watching the wet billows of wind that swept around the corner of the

43

building between him and the lights of the town. There were enough of them to show the main street, sleek and black. He shrugged the coat up until his shoulders were snug in it, then he advanced into the storm. By the time he got to the garage, the walk had warmed him, and the edge was gone from the wind.

The night man came in high rubber boots with a dripping sponge in his hand. He said: 'Yeah?' His young face was frowning.

'Who you got can drive me to Fullerton?' asked O'Rourke.

'Nobody,' said the night man.

'What's your name?'

'McGuire.'

'Sure,' said O'Rourke. 'I knew you were Irish.'

'I'm half German and a quarter Welsh and an eighth French,' said McGuire, beginning to turn away.

'Listen, brother,' said O'Rourke, 'Irish is the oil. No matter what you mix it with, it comes to the top . . .'

McGuire laughed. 'Yeah? All right,' he said. 'Maybe.'

'I'm O'Rourke,' he went on. 'From the headquarters force in New York.'

'The hell you are!'

'Yeah, badge and gun and everything. Wanta see them? How much to take me to Fullerton?'

'And get canned in the morning for leaving the job?'

44

'You couldn't help it. The damned cop made you go.'

'Made me?' growled McGuire. He laughed the frown out of his face. 'All right. You made me go. Twenty bucks?' he added speculatively.

'Twenty dollars,' grunted O'Rourke. But he answered: 'Well, the city's rich ... You know the country all around Fullerton?'

'Do I know the palm of my hand?'

'You know the palm of your hand when there's twenty bucks in it,' said O'Rourke. 'Come on, brother. Let's make a start.'

'Requisition that big sedan over there for us,' suggested McGuire.

'I've already requisitioned it, in the name of the law,' grinned O'Rourke. 'Let's climb.'

The rain smashed the windshield a dusty white with a volley of water as they lurched into the street. The double windshield wipers clicked hurriedly back and forth as the engine raced. Through a pale cone of light they felt their way down the street, a million crystal pencilings slashing across the radiance. They left the street lamps and turned into the emptiness of the open country.

'The station at Fullerton,' said O'Rourke. 'Just below the station, where there's a couple of stacks of ties corded up.'

Distance covered in a train seems a thing that an automobile never will get over, just as distance in an automobile seems something that walking cannot possibly traverse. They got

45

down to Fullerton with a smooth sliding of the big car all the way. Small pools of water kept dashing into spray that rang on the fenders and made muddy clouds across the windshield glass, but McGuire knew his way and got there. At the appointed place he stopped, snapped on a searchlight, and turned its strong shaft slowly across two piles of ties, all tarred and stacked and ready for using.

O'Rourke got out and walked down the tall railroad fence, wondering how much it cost by the rod to fence a double way from New York to Chicago. He did not arrive at figures. He preferred merely to wonder. He crawled through between the rails and began to sweep the ground with his electric torch. A spilling of oil, running blue-green in the rain water, showed him, he thought, where the engine must have stopped. He measured off an approximate distance to the point where the car of John Cobb might have been in the procession. There he began to scan the ground more carefully. Packed cinders do not compress any more easily wet than dry, but in the soft of the ground off the railbed he found tracks. The heel marks sank well in. Grass grew here. Close to the fence the grass was smeared down. It was still springing up as it might have done if a body had been flung down there an hour or so before—flung down and then dragged under the fence.

Here O'Rourke turned around and looked

back toward the rails, conjuring up the picture that had risen in his eyes of a single man carrying a limp weight out from under the staring eyes of light that shone from the train, throwing the weight down here, dragging it calmly under the fence. To be sure, the rain must have obscured everything. Or perhaps the fellow had paused behind the stack of ties. No, there was no confusion of footmarks there. He had gone straight on, defying the eyes of the train. At a certain point in any crime there is a moment when the criminal shows a queer courage, but in this crime he had been brave all the way through. Whether he had acted in cooperation with a confederate inside the train, as Campbell thought, or had worked the entire trick from the outside, by means of that dangling, perilous rope, the fellow had been a hero throughout.

It was not the force of the wind or the rushing weight of the rain that made O'Rourke shiver a little. He crawled through the bars of the fence again, on the trail. It crossed the road through the headlight flung from the waiting car and entered the grass of the field beyond. Stones had been pulled from the top of the fence. They lay inside. He could tell that they had fallen recently because their undersides were less dark colored than the weathered old veterans which topped the wall on either side.

Another thing made O'Rourke stoop with

47

his lantern. On the grass there was sign that a body had fallen here with great weight. It brought into his eyes a picture of an unconscious form dragged by the heels, the head and shoulders allowed to drop brutally from the height of the fence to the ground. If that were the case, John Cobb was dead by this time. Kidnappers cherish their victims. They don't drag them to death.

Why, then, had not Cobb been murdered on the train? Why that frantic desire to get him living from the stateroom and out across country?

O'Rourke, breathing of the mystery, put back his head and regarded the rain which was slashing into his face.

'McGuire,' he called.

The tall fellow came running to him.

'You see this?' said O'Rourke. He pointed his light down on the beaten and dragged grass.

'Yeah. I see.'

'The trail goes on across the meadow,' said O'Rourke. 'I wish you had a gun. I'd like you for company on this little walk.'

'I don't need a gun,' said McGuire. 'I'll go along.'

'Your car is gonna get terribly wet. Maybe this is a dead body that's being dragged through the grass, McGuire. And that car sure is getting wet.'

'Damn the car,' said McGuire.

'The Irish is like oil,' murmured O'Rourke.

It comes right to the top.'

McGuire ran back to the car, snapped off the strong headlights, and put on the meager parking lamps. Then he hurried up to O'Rourke. He was a big-striding fellow, and the tails of his overcoat flapped and snapped around his knees. O'Rourke deliberately put the hand torch straight upon him. The wet, stiff crop of unshaven hair glistened on the face of McGuire. The greasy swipes on his face, which made him seem older, could not disguise the fact, now, that he was hardly more than twenty. The grease on his face and his eyes shone with the same brightness. He had a rounded mug of a face with plenty of bone in the wide jaw.

'I've got something in a pinch,' he said and showed a heavy monkey-wrench. 'If I chuck this into the middle of some guy, it sure is gonna mix up his works for him. He'll stop ticking for a while.' McGuire laughed and brandished the monkey-wrench. 'Let's go,' he said. 'It's not doing nothing that gets a guy down. Leave us see where this jerry was going, anyway.'

The trail was easily followed. That weight which the man had carried from the train appeared to be too great to consider carrying any longer. It was dragged on straight across the grass. The wet of that grass ought to have roused a chloroformed victim from unconsciousness by this time, thought O'Rourke, but now he found the ground descending into a small, sandy gulch with

49

streaks and small pools of water standing in it. The weight had been pulled down one side of this minute ravine, through the middle of a shallow pool, and up the farther side. O'Rourke, when he reached the opposite bank, looked back with his light at the distinctly marked trail.

'Yeah,' said McGuire, 'think of that devil! Was the guy dead that he was hauling?'

'I dunno,' answered O'Rourke.

There were woods before them, naked, dreary, pulling darkness around them from the black earth and the dingy sky. It was a two-power flashlight that he carried, and now O'Rourke turned on the dimmer. Even this he used only from time to time, for they had established the line of flight, and only needed to check it occasionally.

'Suppose this louse is hiding away and taking a peek at us as we come along?' asked McGuire.

'Yeah. Suppose,' agreed O'Rourke.

The rain turned to a gusty drizzling, after a moment. When they were inside the trees, the storm ceased altogether and, through the naked branches, O'Rourke saw the clouds breaking away into massive ranges and mountainous islands that sailed down the sky. The stars looked quietly through from behind.

Still with the dimmer globe of the flashlight O'Rourke led the way. He said: 'You scatter out to the side, McGuire. Supposing he was to

50

let loose, why should he get two birds with one bullet?'

'Yeah, supposing,' echoed McGuire and kept on at his side.

The woods cleared. In the clearing stood a little summer alcove. It could not be called a summer house, because it was not roofed. The hedge and the wattled wall enclosed a small space, and the trail of the dragged weight led directly into the entrance. O'Rourke hesitated half a moment. Then he walked straight in, with McGuire crowding his shoulder in eagerness not to be last.

The furniture of the little summer alcove consisted of green painted iron chairs around an iron table. In one of the chairs sat a lumpish black thing that looked more like a mud image than a man. Fire had melted it out of shape or recognition. All the ground beneath its feet was black, and the strong wires were visible that had bound the body in the chair, motionless. A single feature could be made out: the gape of the mouth, distended by a wire gag.

CHAPTER SEVEN

Seven Faces

After a moment McGuire turned and stumbled out of the place. O'Rourke listened

51

to the retching. He kept on scanning the floor of the summer alcove, for the ground was soft and footmarks were everywhere. But except for one line of easily distinguishable tracks that led straight up to the chair, the rest were muffled pads, and he knew that the murderer had wrapped his feet in rags as he moved about the place.

A glint of metal in the horrible scorched blackness of the lap of the dead had the eye of O'Rourke now. He picked up a thin platinum watch, flaked over with carbon that shook away at once and left the metal almost as pure as though it had just come from a jeweler's case. When he pried the back open he read, inside: 'To John Cobb, from Larry, Bill, and Joe.'

Lawrence Purvis Pelton, that first name would mean, perhaps. Well, Larry would be getting a return for this present before long.

O'Rourke sat down in one of the green painted chairs and lighted a cigar. McGuire came in, green-yellow of face, scowling to keep his courage high.

'Sit down,' said O'Rourke.

'I'll stand up . . . and walk around.'

'You'll do no damn' thing of the kind,' insisted O'Rourke. 'What's written on the floor may be the last chapter of the book of this crime. Sit down. Have a cigar.'

'No!' McGuire refused hastily.

'You're young,' said O'Rourke. A shower of

rain blew out of nowhere, for all overhead seemed starry and bright. 'You're young, and you can't take it. The day'll come when this sort of stuff won't mean nothing. You'll take it easy. This here is a grouch and a grudge murder. Or else maybe it's something else again. Tell me about the folks around here.'

'They're all a high-hat crowd,' said McGuire, sitting stiffly on the edge of his chair and fingering his monkey-wrench nervously.

'Like who?' asked O'Rourke.

'The Crays, and the Loftus family, and the Ginnis crowd . . . they are pretty new . . . and the Willoughbys, and John Cobb has some ground that begins a half mile off and . . .'

'Leave off at John Cobb,' said O'Rourke. 'What sort of a man is he?'

'He's a scrawny kind of a mean guy,' said McGuire. 'He's a nut.'

'How come?'

'He's got millions, but he lives in a little house and does his own work.'

'His own work?'

'It's a little house and has a lot of stunts in it that work by electricity. He does his own laundry, even, partly. The wool socks and all that. He's just a nut. And mean.'

'A millionaire that don't get no fun? I've seen that kind. Mostly half of them are that kind. They dunno what to do. The fun with money is wanting to do something and being scared of going broke. They can't go broke, so they don't have no fun. Cobb must have some friends for neighbors, though?'

'I never heard of none.'

O'Rourke puffed thoughtfully and stared at the blackened and formless body.

'Comes up here, rapped on the head ... likely ... wired into the chair. Gasoline or kerosene poured over him. Lighted ... I read in a book where they used to do that in Rome, in the old days.'

'Mussolini?' asked McGuire.

'Aw, hell no. A long ways back ... you oughta study your history, kid ... it does a lot for a guy ... back when they had martyrs. They'd wrap 'em up and soak 'em in oil and, when Nero wanted to give a bang-up party, he'd have the martyrs lighted, and the yelling they done was the music that Nero ate to. He got fat on it ... The guy that murdered Cobb, he maybe was a reader.'

'Cobb?' cried McGuire.

'I guess it's John Cobb,' said O'Rourke, pointing to the watch. 'There's one part of his name that wasn't burned up, even if the glass of the watch cracked. Funny thing, McGuire, how the fire kind of burned off the rough edges and turned him into black dough, ain't it?'

'Yeah ... funny,' choked McGuire.

'No friends you know about?'

'Nobody I know. He ... is *that* millionaire

John Cobb?' asked the boy again.

'Maybe not,' said O'Rourke. 'One of the big wheezes, these days, is to give your man a ride and then burn him so's nobody'll know about him.'

He stood up and leaned over the dead body again. 'But there's some dental work in his mug that'll help to identify him,' explained O'Rourke. 'It's a wonderful thing how a dentist can be useful, outside of his working hours. Where is Cobb's home?'

'Back down behind the woods a little way.'

'Did Cobb own these woods here?'

'They all put in and owned them. They all put in and bought them when Jefferson Craig died, a year or two back.'

'They take him off the train,' O'Rourke mused aloud, 'and they drag him up here. Why? So's to be done with him, fenced in by trees. Know that Cobb's to die. They hardly care whether they kill him or not on the way. But want to get something out of him before he kicks off. Wire him into the chair. Leave one hand free to make signatures, perhaps? I wonder about that...? Signatures...? Anyway, in the windup, gasoline over the body. Then a match thrown on it. The flame booms. It explodes. After the first rush of the fire, there's our friend, John Cobb, sitting in a welter of the fire and his hair blazin' up like a torch. More gasoline thrown on, maybe, to freshen the flames a good bit. Then the fire burns down, and the job is done. The face of John Cobb has been wiped away. The rain comes bucketing down. And there you are! Neat, McGuire, ain't it?'

McGuire said nothing. It was possible for him to look at the dreadful, gaping, faceless body, but it was not possible for him to utter a sound.

O'Rourke, shifting his cigar to one side of his mouth, crouched on the floor and began to hum as he made a tracing of two of the footprints on the floor of the alcove. He stood up and hummed quietly on with the same monotonous tune.

'Now we start for the Cobb house,' he said, 'if you'll show me the way, McGuire.'

McGuire nodded and rose hastily to leave but, O'Rourke, at the entrance to the alcove, didn't feel the clayish loam underfoot but rather the gritting of sand. He took a kick at it, for it lay in a little mound, but it concealed nothing apparently. So he went on behind McGuire.

The flashlight showed them their way through the woods. It was largely of birches, and their trunks flashed as white as chalk.

'It's ghostly, damned if it ain't,' said McGuire, gripping his monkey-wrench hard.

'Yeah,' said O'Rourke, stumbling over an exposed root, 'whenever there's been a dead man in your eye, it keeps you thinking for a few minutes afterward. It's funny, that way. I dunno why.'

McGuire looked at him so hard that he stumbled in his turn. They came out from the woods onto a winding path that led to a road, and by the starlight O'Rourke could see the big houses that sat far back from the highway, swelling fronts, avenues, and cloudy groves of trees.

'All kind of high hat, eh?' said O'Rourke.

'High as hell,' agreed McGuire. 'Here's the entrance to Cobb's place . . . Mister O'Rourke, was it him, back there, you think?'

'I guess it was him, all right,' said O'Rourke, 'but I won't be sure till the dentist has a look.'

They turned into the driveway for the panels of the iron gate were open. It was almost half a mile to the house. When O'Rourke saw it, he said: 'A hundred thousand dollars' worth of land and a two-thousand-dollar shack on it?'

He looked across the easy slope and down to the shadowy Hudson which took a bend here, big and still as a lake.

'The house ain't big, but they say that he spent fifty thousand on it,' said McGuire.

'Newspaper dollars,' said O'Rourke. 'How could you get fifty thousand bucks into a dump the size of that unless you stuck a lot of gold leaf on the walls?'

'How'll we get in?' asked McGuire. 'You gotta key?'

'We'll get in, all right,' said O'Rourke. And he laughed a little.

He tried the front and back door first, as a matter of course. Both were locked. There was no shed, no barn, no outhouse of any sort near the little building. The doors and windows were small. It was like a section of a ship, stuck up here on the top of the slope like a look-out. Perhaps that was what it was—a look-out. O'Rourke registered the idea in his mind for future reference.

He tried windows after that, but they were fast, every one, and nothing but great force could pry them up. He had to pick up a rock and shatter a pane before he could reach up and turn the catch. Then he pushed up the window slowly and leaned into the interior, for the sill was surprisingly close to the ground. His flashlight showed him a small dining room, the furniture old mahogany. The walls were paneled with dark carved wood. The whole room had a satiny gleam of care and richness.

'Yeah ... maybe fifty thousand ... Jeez,' said O'Rourke, and climbed through the window. McGuire followed him. When O'Rourke turned the electric switch, the room shone with light from four small wall-brackets. At the same time a horrible clamor of alarm bells made McGuire jump.

'Burglar alarms and everything,' grinned O'Rourke, turning off the switch.

But the racket continued and seemed to grow.

'Let's get out of here,' suggested McGuire.

'It's only some noise. Nobody can hear it on the road,' said O'Rourke. 'How does noise make any difference?'

He pushed through to the next room which was the kitchen. It was as small as a galley on a boat and as conveniently arranged. White tiles covered the walls to the ceiling. The electric stove was white tiled, also. The whole room had an arctic glare like snow. Several wires were plugged into one big fixture in a corner. O'Rourke tried them one by one and finally pulled out one that silenced the alarm. The silence began to walk in upon them by degrees. McGuire could breathe again.

'Look it,' he said. 'There's the electric washing machine. There's the slot window that lets the clothes line run outside into the sun. Vacuum cleaner, floor polisher, everything electric and all handy.'

'Yeah. Fifty thousand bucks, maybe,' said O'Rourke. 'It's funny, ain't it? Living up here like a bird on a damn' branch so's the hawks couldn't come near to him.'

He went on into a combination living room-library with the same low ceiling that closed the other rooms of the house. The big fireplace filled almost the entire end of the chamber. Bookcases filled every other wall space. O'Rourke walked slowly past them. The great majority were detective stories and serious books on crime and criminals. There were, also, a few volumes on mineralogy. Nothing else was on the shelves.

It was a very bright, cheery room, the floor overlaid from end to end with Persian rugs which were not fitted side to side but overlapped in a luxurious confusion and gave the floor a wavering, uneven level.

O'Rourke pushed on to the fourth and last room of the little house. It was the largest of all, this bedchamber, with the bed fitted into a wall alcove so that it projected hardly at all into the floor space. Another big fireplace insured the winter comfort of John Cobb. Between this and the bathroom there was an enlarged closet, or dressing room, with one small, high window. Light, cloth-covered doors kept the series of clothes poles from dust. John Cobb was a fellow who thought a good deal of his appearance. There must have been fifty or sixty suits for all occasions. What O'Rourke reached for was a pair of tan shoes on the high rack which contained so many. He studied them with care for a moment and then drew from his pocket the outlines he had made of the tracks in the summer alcove among the trees. When he fitted the shoes over these impressions they were in exact accord. The heel was of just the right breadth and depth, the toe-curve precisely the same.

'Yeah,' said O'Rourke, rising from his knees, 'that was John Cobb that burned to death in that chair.'

'Why?' said McGuire. 'He never done

nothing to nobody around here.'

'There's fifteen million reasons why,' said O'Rourke.

He stood back and glanced around the room. There was one very odd, distinguishing feature of the place, and that was the series of large photographs attached to the cloth coverings of the closet doors. There were seven of these doors, and on each was affixed a big picture of a man. The dearest friends or associates of John Cobb, no doubt.

'But you wouldn't think,' said O'Rourke, 'that a lonely mug like this fellow would care that much about his pals, would you?'

'He didn't care nothing about people,' said McGuire.

'How d'you know that?' asked O'Rourke.

'Me? Oh, I've seen his face . . . I've seen him with people. They didn't matter to him.'

'We'll go down to the cellar and the garage,' said O'Rourke. 'If these ain't his friends, why would he have their pictures around?'

Here his eye stopped on one of the portraits. It was of a lad of twenty, perhaps, a big fellow in a flannel shirt open at the throat with a shadow of unshaven whiskers on his face. The likeness was excellent, and O'Rourke recognized instantly the face of Charles Latimer.

CHAPTER EIGHT

One of the Hunted

Angus Campbell took his thin face and his ferret's eye into the state-room from which the passenger had disappeared so mysteriously. In it was coiled the entire length of the rope which had been dangling outside the window, and this rope he now passed and repassed through his hands, thoughtfully, often pausing to look again at the three-pronged grappling iron at the end of the length. The grapple was made of the finest steel, drawn to points exquisitely fine. A three-taloned claw like this would have fixed its foot at the first grasp on a surface of sheer, polished granite. Easily it would bite into the metal roof of the car. It could be thrown up from the ground and, the moment it caught hold, the weight of a man's body as he climbed up the side of the car would be ample to work the sharp teeth into the steel above for a secure hold. This much was explained, therefore. He felt that he had in his hands one of the fundamentals of the crime, because it was his experience that the fundamentals always are simple things. If you have the dagger that killed the king, the rest ought to be fairly easy. By this rope, felt

Campbell, he might draw the criminal to the electric chair, while O'Rourke, like the fat-headed Irish fool that he was, blundered through rain and mud on a trail that had no meaning.

Campbell, at this point, drew a deep breath of relief and pulled from his pocket a little round reading glass that magnified a number of times. With this he started to go over the stateroom inch by inch. He had neither hope nor doubt as he worked. His chief concern was to move as little as possible so that sign of Campbell would not complicate the other sign in the stateroom. Into it had come, so far as he knew, O'Rourke, the porter, that big Charles Latimer, the vanished man from the stateroom, and Campbell.

Too many people, thought Campbell, as he dropped on his knees and surveyed the floor. He found there some large dabs of cigar ashes, one of them half an inch long and almost perfectly intact. One of O'Rourke's cigars, of course. Yet O'Rourke had not been in the stateroom any great length of time which made the presence of that ash rather a mystery. He found the butt end of a cigar, a considerable section bitten off with great force which had squashed the soft of the tobacco leaf together. This small treasure Campbell wrapped in a little twist of paper and put into a vest pocket. Yonder there was a considerable gray smear of the cigar ashes, and in it remained fairly clearly

63

the print of the foot which had spread the mark. The shoe had a delicately pointed tip. It was a woman's shoe that must have made the mark.

Here Campbell sat back on his heels and grunted softly. For his spirit was being fed. No woman, so far as he knew, could have entered the stateroom, yet the sign was there, as clear as a photograph and a signed confession of her presence. He rocked forward to examine the mark again. The heel print was not close to the mark of the toe, which indicated one of two things—either that she was a very large woman or that she wore low heels. Campbell traced the imprint very much as O'Rourke, not very much later, was to trace the mark of the man's shoe in that summer alcove.

When this had been done with accuracy, Campbell continued his laborious examination of the floor of the stateroom. He even picked up and preserved in his twist of thin paper several hairs which he discovered. His search now climbed to the seats.

People leave different marks on plush. Men sit with their legs at different angles; their weight depresses the plush nap more or less. Sometimes minute particles of the cloth from their trousers may be recovered. But though Campbell squinted from one side and then from another, he gained nothing at all assured as testimony. He swung his notice now to the walls. On the merest suggestion of a rough splinter-base near the door, shoulder high, he discovered a very fine white thread—a spider thread, no more. But that, no doubt, was where the porter had rubbed against the wall.

He imprisoned that thread in one of his paper twists. It meant nothing, perhaps. Indeed, single things are not apt to have much meaning, but when four or five of the insignificant details are laid side by side, they begin to make sense.

Continuing to the windows, he discovered one of the screws of the window frame had worked loose, slightly. Just enough to catch under the sharp edge of its head a little tuft of brownish thread. Campbell rolled it into a thread. A brownish thread such as might have come out of the fabric of a loosely woven tweed.

That was when he remembered big Charles Latimer, huge Charles Latimer who had battered in the door with the massive weight of his shoulder. Yet Latimer, so far as he knew, had not sat down on one of the seats. Instead, he had still been on the move until the stateroom was cleared out by the detectives. No person, standing, could have rubbed away that little airy tuft of material. It was impossible. Campbell, taking his place on the seat, made sure that the scrap of thread was actually higher than his own shoulder. He had to raise himself three inches to bring his shoulder in line. Then he rubbed his shoulder forward across the screwhead.

From his own gray tweed coat nothing detached. It was a much larger man than he who had sat there, a bulky, ponderous man whose body movements had mass behind them. The more he thought of it, the more certain it was that the fellow must be Charles Latimer, who had been so readily at hand when O'Rourke wanted that door broken down.

* * *

Campbell, having completed his examination as far as the suitcases stacked in the racks above the seats, relaxed and sat down for a smoke. He needed the soothing breath of tobacco now, and he drew down the smoke deep into his narrow lungs. The suitcases could wait until the end of the trip. In Chicago he would go through them in detail, bit by bit, with whatever legal examiner might be assigned to the case. Besides, in the disappearance of the passenger, this luggage probably was of no importance. Otherwise the essential part of it would have been taken along. For the brain which had conceived and executed this work, Campbell was sure, was a masterful intelligence incapable of overlooking important details. However, such things as little tufts of cloth scraped off on the head of a screw may be magnified into the ropes which hang the guilty.

He left the stateroom and went back into the lounge car. Most people had gone to bed by this time. Four men sat in at a resolved rubber of bridge. The wife of one of them had come in to deal a few icy words to her husband. He was accepting them with his jaws hard set, his cigar raking at an upward angle, his endurance near the breaking point.

Also, in the lounge, big Charles Latimer sat talking with that incredibly lovely girl. There was the tall man with the black beard and the full, red mouth and the eyebrows arched in eternal surprise. Two others, sleepily finishing drinks and reading, made up the list in the lounge car. The detective left them and went back down the train. He roused each porter in turn, as he entered the cars, to ask briefly: 'Got a big man, around thirty years, brownish tweed suit . . . damn' big over all . . . smiling sort of a fellow?'

At last he found the right porter who declared that Charles Latimer had a compartment in that car. A glimpse of the detective's badge roused the porter past yawning. His frightened eyes rolled sidewise as he fitted the key into the door and opened the compartment. Campbell waved him out and surveyed the scene when he was left alone. On the wall hung a huge raincoat with a buttoned-in fleece lining. The only bag was a massive pigskin affair, well battered and time worn. He opened it and slipped a tentative hand down among the clothes until his fingertips touched metal. He passed his left hand down, lifted the clothes, and drew out a work-size forty-five caliber Colt. Campbell fingered it before he replaced it, making sure that it fitted exactly into the niche which its weight had hollowed out among the clothes. After that, he left the compartment and the wide-eyed porter.

He returned to the lounge car and ordered a Scotch, neat. Why good whiskey should be qualified with water or siphon he never had been able to understand. Its strength was its beauty, and a man who knew how to sip could make the drink last even longer than with an addition of seltzer. Campbell was one who knew how to sip.

The beautiful girl and Charles Latimer were the objects of his side-long regard for some time, until he made sure that she was wearing low heels, which set well back from the toes of her shoes and made her slender feet seem rather long. It was by no means a complete system of observations and deductions, but it was enough to assure Campbell that the girl had been in the stateroom before the kidnapping.

The girl and Charles Latimer. Both had been there, perhaps at the same time. He had the strength to handle a slender fellow like the missing man. He could have thrown Cobb out the window like a ball. And the cold, calm

68

profile of the girl, hardly warmed by her smiling, told Campbell that she might be capable of almost anything. He knew our 20th-Century women by heart, he told himself. Whatever men would do, the woman might attempt also.

The big fellow with the red mouth and the black beard was lighting a fresh cigar, turning it slowly between his lips with one hand while with half-closed eyes he puffed, drawing the flame from the match. An odor of a peculiar rankness reached the nostrils of Campbell, and he was so irritated that he went out on the platform at the end of the lounge car and watched the stars like sparks whirling in from the two horizons, and the dark of the trees on one side drawing toward the gleam of the river on the other. The shrill of the wind blew a flute note beside his ears. The clicking of the wheels kept up a broken rhythm under the train, a sort of crazy, conversational muttering.

Absently he fumbled at the little twists of paper in his vest pocket. The biggest pinch of all was the fragment which had been bitten from the butt of the cigar. He took this out, cut it in two, impaled it on the end of his pocket knife, and held the flame of his cigarette lighter to it, until the tobacco glowed. Afterwards he inhaled the fumes. The heart of Campbell sickened in him then leaped away in a rioting joy of speculation. For he had recognized, beyond a doubt, the same odor which had driven him impatiently from the lounge car. He flicked the bit of cigar from the blade of the knife, closed it with a snap, and sauntered back into the car.

'Different, eh?' said Campbell, pausing beside the chair of Aloysius Grosvenor. 'Not the kind of cigars that most people smoke, eh?'

Grosvenor looked up and smiled first at Campbell and then at the ash which was forming at the end of his smoke, a light gray ringed with dark circles. Campbell, also, was studying that ash with a hungry interest.

'I import 'em from Puerto Rico,' lied Grosvenor. 'You got to have a taste to enjoy 'em. You got to have a real taste . . . Try one?'

'Thanks,' said Campbell, gratefully. 'I'll try it after dinner tomorrow. Thanks very much.'

He strolled back onto the platform at the end of the train and watched the whirling stars again. He could not help thinking of O'Rourke, off there in the darkness, in the mud, following his nose to confusion like the Irish idiot that he was. O'Rourke, complacent, self-contented, at ease with himself, already thinking up smart cracks to pass along to Corrigan at the end of this case. But the real mystery, Campbell knew, accompanied him upon this train.

No wonder that the cigar smoker and Latimer and the girl were all in the lounge car.

No wonder at all, because it began to come to Campbell that all three of them were working together.

The more he brooded upon the thing, the more real it was to him. Not one of the three was a usual type. Criminals who plotted the kidnapping of a person as wealthy as John Cobb were sure to be out of the ordinary run. Let O'Rourke do something for his half of the job and he, Campbell, would guarantee to work out the other portion on the train. At last they might emerge with truth perfect and whole, like the fitted halves of an apple.

He was cutting out a portion of the butt of Grosvenor's cigar, as he passed these thoughts through his mind. Just as he had lighted the other fragment, so he lighted this on the end of his knife blade, and ignited it with a touch of flame. Afterward he inhaled the foul aroma with more pleasure than any connoisseur ever felt when breathing of the most exquisite bouquet of some rare old Burgundy or an attentively ripened vintage of the Rhine.

For it told him, definitely, that Grosvenor had dropped that cigar butt in the stateroom of John Cobb. The whole thing was welding together. The girl, too pretty to be true, big Charles Latimer with the gun in his case, and yonder red-lipped cigar smoker—all were working together as a closed corporation. They had seen to it that the helpless, chloroformed body of Cobb was passed out the window of the stateroom to confederates posted outside. The thing was as clear as pure glass. It was perfect.

As he snapped the glowing bit of tobacco from the knife end into the dark where the wind streaked it away into a straight gleaming line, Campbell felt something behind him. No one had come through the door since he had stepped onto the platform, and yet he felt an essence, as it were, standing immediately behind him, casting a chill of danger into the air.

He wondered, suddenly, why more people had not been tapped over the head and dropped on the rails from the observation platform train. All token of the blow would be rubbed out by the smashing force of the fall, of course.

Campbell turned suddenly and saw through the glass of the door the foreign face of the man with the black beard and the red lips. The naïve bend of the brows seemed at that moment the arch malice of a superior fiend, and the eyes seemed to Campbell dangerous fires.

Aloysius Grosvenor turned away and strolled back to his seat. He left Campbell wondering what conclusion, if any, could be deduced from a glimpse of a fellow standing in seclusion and sniffing the fumes that rose from the burning of a bit of cigar? Perhaps there had been no threat, no awareness whatever in

72

the eyes of the big fellow, but Campbell kept a chill in the small of his back for long moments afterward. It was, in fact, a familiar sensation, for he had spent a great part of his life feeling like a hunting cat, or like one of the hunted.

CHAPTER NINE

Enter Pete

In the living room of John Cobb's house O'Rourke lingered before going down to the garage. Considering the tidy habits of this man, it was impossible that he should have left the place before locking up everything securely, and O'Rourke wanted the keys.

He found them, or a duplicate bunch, in one of the little drawers at the top of the desk. The largest of the lot might well open the garage. McGuire, while this examination went on, stood in the center of the room, dripping silence, looking from one door toward another as though they were guns pointed at his head. He was a little pale, but his eyes were bright.

O'Rourke, after a measuring glance at him, led the way out of the house again. The wind that had rolled the clouds out of the sky and burnished the stars was blowing warmer than ever. The grass crunched, soggy with wet,

73

under their feet as they made the turn of the house and found the concrete path which led to the garage door. The torch of O'Rourke swept the face of the door and centered on the lock. Into it, as he had expected, the largest key fitted neatly. So new, so good was the condition of everything, the bolt slid without a sound, and one wide panel of the door swung gently open. O'Rourke sent the gleam of the torch before him over the oily pavement of the room. A far stronger blast of light smote him at once in the face, blinding him.

A voice said: 'Just step right in, gentlemen. Put up your hands and step right in and make yourselves at home, will you?'

O'Rourke could see the gun clearly, not the man behind it. That figure was a stodgy sketch of blackness, a dark overcoat, a hat smudged in above the mere gleam of a face, where the powerful ray of the man's pocket torch beat down the feeble blade of O'Rourke's light. The sketch of a man that O'Rourke made out might have stood for murder on the jacket on any ancient dime novel, but the gun, which was clearly seen, was the very essence of modernity, a big, cruelly efficient automatic. The light which he used was ultra-modern also. The big orb of it included easily the forms of both O'Rourke and McGuire.

O'Rourke had not hesitated in putting up his hands. It was the sight of the steady gun that gave him the order, not the words.

The fellow added: 'I mean you, too . . . and don't be a fool!'

McGuire, at the shoulder of O'Rourke, at last got his hands up. Beside O'Rourke he made two steps into the garage. The indescribable sour, thin pungency of gasoline was in the air now as they entered well into the chamber. Heating pipes passed over the low ceiling. Through an open door they had a glimpse—by O'Rourke's torch—of another bit of the cellar, the furnace, its gauges, its big, round, octopus arms wriggling away above. It seemed big enough to supply motive power— to put this nautical bit of a house in motion.

'Right on with you,' said the master of the situation. 'Keep your faces toward the back wall. March ahead!'

They were passing this commander when something happened that O'Rourke did not see, except as a rush of shadows from the corner of his eye. Something swept up suddenly from the floor—McGuire's foot. It struck the gun out of the hand that threatened them. There was an explosion. A whiff of death went past the face of O'Rourke and left his soul trembling in its wake. The gun clanged on the floor a split part of a second after McGuire wrapped his long, powerful arms around the man in the dark, for the other's torch had clicked on the pavement and gone out.

O'Rourke turned his gun and his own light

on the struggle. It was over already. One of McGuire's strangling arms had tipped back the hat of the stranger from a gray head of hair and from one of those seven faces which O'Rourke had looked at on the doors in Cobb's dressing room. The fellow was nearing sixty, perhaps. His thin hands wrenched hopelessly at the muscular arms of McGuire. He was making an altogether vague effort to strike upwards with his knee.

'I guess that's all, McGuire,' said O'Rourke.

The lad stepped back, still keeping his great hands on the other, and panting with hunger. The terror was still in him, shaking him, the sort of frantic madness of fear that makes some men perform what cold courage would shrink from. His mouth was partly open. His lips quivered. He looked as though he wished to get his teeth in.

'I didn't see . . .,' he said, 'I didn't see that he was such a skinny old man.'

O'Rourke stood behind the captive and rested the muzzle of his gun in the small of the fellow's back.

'Just go through him, McGuire,' he said. 'Get everything. Then we'll have a talk. He looks like the sort of a mug that could tell a good yarn.'

The mug had a sunburned face, long, thin, above what had once been a mighty neck, though now so withered that the substructure showed through the big cords and the lean of the muscles, dented at the nape where time first taps a strong man with the edge of her hand and makes the first of her marks. Though the hair was gray, the eyebrows remained black and gave a touch of grimness to the expression. Under the brows, strange to say, were eyes that should have gone with a blond complexion. They were auburn eyes, small, very youthfully bright. He was about a middle height. Once he had been a powerful specimen but the years had stripped away ten or fifteen vital pounds of meat.

McGuire, going through the pockets, laid on the workbench that ran along a side of the room a small comb in a case of worn leather, a pipe whose first mouthpiece had been broken or chewed away so that a fresh tooth grip had been nicked into the stem, a billfold given away by an insurance company with the name of the company in gilt letters on the imitation leather, a handkerchief of thick, cheap cotton, a pocket knife with a horn handle that was cracked away from the steel of the frame at one end, two slips of paper matches, one partly used, and a sack of cigarette tobacco with a thin sheaf of wheatstraw papers to go with it. The papers were held inside blue cardboard sides by a bit of elastic string. There was an old rubber tobacco pouch to accommodate the pipe, a twist of string, another and larger twist of twine, new, strong, and good, half a dozen loose cartridges for the automatic, forty-five caliber, seventy-five cents in silver and three one-dollar bills, four fives, three fifties, five hundreds. Also there was a neat pocket kit hardly larger than a matchbox containing needles of three sizes, white and black thread, pins, safety pins, a thimble, and a dozen buttons.

O'Rourke turned the billfold inside out. No name, no initials were in it. He turned out the collar of the man's coat. The name of the maker had been clipped out neatly.

'We better go up and sit down,' said O'Rourke. 'Pick up that torch and that gun. Gather up all this stuff and come along after us, son, will you? You and me are gonna have to have quite a little talk, eh?' he added to the prisoner.

'Why, sure,' said the older man. 'Why not, anyway?'

'Go out in front of me,' said O'Rourke. 'Remember that I've got the light on you, and I'm nudging you in the back every minute with the muzzle of this gun. Just keep that in mind, and we oughta go and have a nice comfortable time. I seen some liquor back there in the pantry. Pinch bottles, brother.'

'Ah, that's my kind of meat,' said the man with the auburn eyes.

'What'll I call you?' asked McGuire.

'Pete, they mostly call me,' he answered.

'All right, Pete. March along, will you? No funny gags?'

'What kind of funny gags could I try?' asked Pete and laughed a little, his lips curling up to show long, narrow, yellow-edged teeth. He went on: 'Once I'm caught, I make a mighty quiet pet. Women like to have me around the house and all that.' He even added: 'That's why I shot so high in the air, when the lad made the swipe at me. I didn't want to puncture the two of you.'

'Did you shoot high in the air?' asked O'Rourke, blinking a little. 'All right. Go right ahead now, and we'll soon be in comfortable chairs.'

He guided Pete out of the garage and around the corner of the house onto the lawn. Pete stumbled and almost went down.

'Kind of slippery,' he said.

'You damned near slipped into hell, that time,' said O'Rourke. 'Watch your step.'

'You bet,' answered old Pete cheerfully and went steadily on until they were almost at the entrance door of the house. Then he dropped down again but continued the same movement, turning it into a swooping turn, while he struck out backhanded at O'Rourke.

McGuire, seeing this from behind, came up with a shout.

'It's all right,' said O'Rourke. 'He won't try it again for a while.'

CHAPTER TEN

Report to Corrigan

They got a fire lighted in the living room fireplace. The flames threw a soft, comfortable bloom over everything, including gray-headed Pete, now with a big lump raised at the edge of his hair.

O'Rourke said: 'I'm going to get some liquor and stuff and bring it in. Will you watch Pete, McGuire?'

'Sure I'll watch him. I'm watching him now.'

'You're not watching him a damned bit. You can't watch him with your eyes. Watch him with a gun.'

'You wanta look out for me,' said Pete, winking one of his strange, auburn-colored eyes at McGuire. 'I might step up and knock you flat and throw you away and skin out!'

McGuire laughed. 'Yeah, maybe you might,' he said.

'I know he looks old and weak,' said O'Rourke. 'But keep that gun on him, will you?'

'All right,' said McGuire, sobering.

O'Rourke left the room. He found the telephone in the pantry first and rang the operator.

'Give me the coroner,' he said.

He heard the gasp of the girl and enjoyed it. He licked his lips and bit the end of a cigar before he was connected. He talked with the cigar in his mouth, the end of it wobbling up and down as he spoke.

'Yes? Yes?' grunted a sleepy voice.

'They've got a dead man sitting up here in the woods,' said O'Rourke. 'Wanta see him? He's pretty.'

'Well? Where?' asked the coroner without enthusiasm. 'Why in hell can't people sit down and die in the daytime? Where is he?'

'Up here in the woods near the Cobb place. You know where that summer alcove is?'

'I know. Got the name of this party?'

'John Cobb,' said O'Rourke and hung up on the cry of astonishment.

He liked this moment of his work. He liked the thought of what might pass through the brain of the coroner when he saw the blackened, horrid mass of flesh which was left of Cobb.

He rang Corrigan. 'Yeah,' groaned Corrigan, and O'Rourke could almost hear the creaking of the bed springs as the big man turned in his bed: 'Yeah . . . O'Rourke! I didn't tell you to wake me up with any damned reports. Where you phoning from? Buffalo?'

'No,' said O'Rourke, 'that guess is wrong.'

'Why in hell should I guess? If you ain't in Buffalo, where does the train stop?'

'Oh, I ain't on the train,' said O'Rourke.

81

He relished the situation. He lighted his cigar and spread his elbows at the board of this crime, as it were. He rejoiced as though in some peculiar virtue.

'I know you ain't on the train,' shouted Corrigan, 'or you couldn't be telephoning. Where are you?'

'I'm in Cobb's house, out here on the Hudson. Nice little place, Corrigan. Ever been out here?'

'You *are* drunk,' said Corrigan. 'You mean that Cobb left the train and went home?'

'He left the train all right,' said O'Rourke.

'Go on. Go on. If you've got anything to say, let me have it. Where's Cobb?'

'In hell,' said O'Rourke.

'What?'

'Unless he bought wings, he couldn't get to a better place, could he?' asked O'Rourke. 'Real skunk, ain't he?'

'O'Rourke, are you tryin' to make a damned fool of me?'

'I'm only telling you something, Inspector. I'm respectfully reporting that John Cobb left the train.'

'You mean he disappeared?'

'I mean he was out of sight for a while after he left the train.'

'And you've got no idea where he is?'

'Sure I've got an idea,' said O'Rourke, 'I can tell you right where he's sitting.'

'Put him on the phone,' said Corrigan. 'I

want to talk to him. Does he think that he can give the New York Police Department the merry old run around like this?'

'I can't get him to the phone right now,' said O'Rourke. 'He's sitting in an iron chair, gagged, and tied up with wire.'

'The hell he is! O'Rourke, what are you talking about?'

'And the face is burnt off of him,' said O'Rourke. 'He's as dead as burned cork, Inspector, and that's what he looks like.'

'Murdered, eh?' asked the inspector.

'Unless he tied himself up and gagged himself, and poured gasoline all over himself, and then touched a match to it. If he didn't do all those things, then somebody else murdered him. I kind of hold out for the murder theory. What about you?'

'Stop this damned nonsense!' shouted Corrigan. 'O'Rourke, what happened?'

'We had a regular dead watch on him. Going to see him every half hour. He wouldn't let us stay in the stateroom with him. Scared to be alone . . . scared to be with us . . . just a yella dog with the color leakin' out all over him. Train gets an emergency stop signal, eases up, and a few minutes later I go back and take a look, and the door's locked. Break it down. Cobb's gone through the window. Chloroform bottle on the floor. Rope hangin' from the top of the train where the thugs crawled down and fished out Cobb. Leave Campbell on the train because the poor Scotch dummy says that the kidnappers, or a part of 'em, must still be on board . . . says it must've been an inside job. He goes on to make the report in Chicago, anyway. I got off the train at the next stop, take a car back, find where a body's been dragged from where the train stopped, go up that trail to where John Cobb sits on an iron chair burned to bits. Watch and shoe prints to identify. Go on to his house. Find a mug there in the garage. I'm right in the middle of the game now. I thought you'd wanna know.'

'This is the damnedest thing I ever heard of,' said the inspector. 'If they wanted to murder him, why didn't they do it on the train and then get themselves out of the way?'

'They wanted to be alone with him,' suggested O'Rourke. 'They wanted to get something out of him, maybe . . . wait a minute . . .'

For he felt, rather than heard, some strange sound or impact in the next room. It was less than a whisper. It was a mere pulse along the nerves, but O'Rourke believed in intuition more than any fat dowager. He got out of his chair with a noiseless speed, stepping on the edges of his soles until he was able to push open, softly, the door to the living room.

McGuire sat where he had been before but with his head lolling back, his mouth open, his eyes closed, except for one glazed and fishy slit. His long, powerful arms hung towards the

84

floor. A knife thrust through the heart might have collapsed that strong machine and left it a worthless litter like this.

Pete was not in sight. Before his empty chair a cigarette still fumed in an ash tray, sending up a white, wavering column that was like a human ghost to O'Rourke. He pushed a little forward until his glance passed over the davenport, over the table in the corner, over a glimmering, colorful mass of books on the shelves, and so to the hall that led a few steps to the front door.

Down that hall it seemed to O'Rourke he saw a shadow disappear. Pete, perhaps, gliding swiftly to take shelter against the wall and then shoot O'Rourke full of lead if he pursued. O'Rourke's face grew as cold and wet as though ice water had been sprayed upon it. He was touched with nausea and seemed to taste, in an instant, all the cigars of the last month. He could see the obscure headline above a small column in an inside newspaper page:

VETERAN DETECTIVE MURDERED IN DESERTED COUNTRY HOUSE

For a tenth of a second he saw that picture. For another tenth part he realized bitterly that he always had had this coming to him. He always let the bloodhound instinct carry him away like the Irish fool that he was. It would have been enough, after all, to report the kidnapping of John Cobb from the train. That would have been sufficient, and then on to Chicago to testify, and so safely back to New York again, living on the fat of the land all the way, instead of tramping through mud from the sight of murder to his own death. The bullet would slap him down. It would smack him in the face. He never had doubted that that would be his ending.

For two tenths of a second O'Rourke hung in his tracks while the electric devil in his brain conjured up the certainty of disaster. Campbell, the lucky Scotch hound, would be finishing a highball at about this hour. O'Rourke moved, and the movement surprised him. Once, when he was a novice on the force, he had said to an old-timer: 'How can you do it? When they got guns and everything, how can you do it?'

The veteran had replied: 'I dunno. You get used to having things expected of you. You're always scared to do something, but you always do it. Something puts a fist in the small of your back and shoves you.'

So O'Rourke, by that impulse of ghostly Roman discipline, was thrust forward from the safe narrow of the doorway to the deadly open space of the room, gliding across it so crouched over that the bigness of his stomach became a constraint. With the last step he leaned well to the right so that he had a view of the hallway. The gray head of Pete glistened there, Pete, with a hand stretched out and resting on the knob of the front door, his body still tip-toed from the effort of lightening the last step. The weight of the big automatic dragged down his right hand.

O'Rourke held him in the gunsights steadily, and that steadiness permitted his heart to beat again, so that a rush of warm, kind blood poured back through his brain and body.

'All right, I've got you,' he said.

Pete, putting down his foot with a half step made, waited silently.

'Chuck down the gun,' said O'Rourke. 'Don't even budge a hair on your head till you chuck down that gun.'

Pete said: 'I can't help the hairs on my head. They're all standing straight up by themselves.' Then he laughed a little at his own joke.

Of all the strange things that O'Rourke had seen and heard in his unusual life, this was the very strangest of all.

'If you try to dodge around at me, I'm gonna saw you right in two, brother,' said O'Rourke.

'Don't you do that,' Pete's calm voice answered, and he threw the gun in front of him.

It fell with a great bang on the floor, slithered into a corner, and turned so that it pointed its big, black mouth at O'Rourke. He had a chilly feeling that it might explode of its

87

own accord.

'Gonna parade me for a while, or do I turn around?' asked Pete.

'Turn around,' ordered O'Rourke and, as Pete swung about slowly, the detective heard something stir in the room behind him, stir, grow large, advance.

He flashed a glance over his shoulder and saw big McGuire risen from his chair with his arms still dangling senselessly and the looseness of death still in his face.

'Hey, McGuire!' he called, staring back at Pete again. 'What's the matter? What happened?'

The wits seemed to return instantly to McGuire as he answered: 'That gray-headed hellion . . . where is he?'

'Step up, Pete,' commanded O'Rourke.

Pete advanced, remarking: 'I hated to do it, young fella. I sure hated to hang it on you, but it seemed like the smart thing to do.'

McGuire walked up to him with his right hand fitting itself carefully into the shape of a hard fist.

'If you were twenty years younger and twenty pounds bigger,' said McGuire, 'I would certainly smash in that dirty mug of yours!'

Pete slipped a hand up over his features and nodded.

'Yeah, maybe,' he said. His thoughtful eyes kept surveying the body of McGuire with something more than a reasonable doubt.

'We were just sitting there, me holding the gun on him,' said McGuire, 'when he reaches out his hand and says, "Wait a minute. You got something on your face." "Spider?" I says, thinking about the cellar we been in, and I sort of stuck my head out for him, and he rapped me.'

He touched a bruised place over his temple.

'It's an old gag,' said Pete, 'but maybe you've noticed how many times the old gags work?' He smiled confidingly at O'Rourke.

The detective said: 'Take that twine and tie him into his chair, McGuire. Tie him good, while I watch.'

So he watched, while McGuire, muttering, lashed his man into the chair.

Pete merely said: 'I thought I'd be out in the open a pretty good ways before that cigarette burned out.'

McGuire, with a consenting nod, went back to the telephone. The voice of Corrigan was yelling impatiently over the wire.

'Aw, slack up a minute, will you?' said O'Rourke. 'I had to leave the phone a minute. The man we caught just rapped my buddy out here and started off. But he's back in harness now. Take it easy, Inspector, and before I'm through with this deal, I'm gonna have the dog-gonedest story that you ever heard.'

He hung up.

CHAPTER ELEVEN

Third Degree

O'Rourke stood in front of the fire, sagging from one foot to the other. 'You're a tough mug, Pete,' he said finally, looking at the man. 'Suppose you tell me how we happened to find you in here? In the garage, down there?'

'That's a funny thing,' Pete mused.

'I'll bet it is,' agreed O'Rourke.

'I was hoofing it down the road,' said Pete. 'Poker always was my long suit, and I'd made a pretty good killing, for me, up the line. But I thought some of the boys might get to thinking, afterwards, that the way I filled two kings to that pair of aces was a little funny. So I didn't travel by railroad. I just cut across country and was pretty tired when I came along here this afternoon . . . late. House kind of stood off comfortable by itself, so I rambled around it and found the garage door unlocked. I went in and was looking around when a fellow came down and took the car out, with me hiding back in the engine room. He drove the car out, and he locked the door behind him . . . and there I was. I tried to get up into the house, but the door was locked at the head of the stairs, too. So I settled down to wait, and

90

dog-gone me, I sure thought that nobody would ever come.'

'What sort of a looking man was the fellow that drove the car away?' asked the detective.

'I didn't get a fair look at him. He was wearing a pretty dark suit, black or blue. He had a narrowish sort of a face and a short black mustache, like he might've been a foreigner . . . Frenchman, or an Italian, or . . .'

'What part of the country you come from?' O'Rourke queried.

Pete crossed his feet. 'Well,' he said, 'that's pretty hard to say. Where I was born, and where I was raised, and where I been living is all different.'

'Born?' asked O'Rourke.

'Alabama.'

'Raised?'

'Kentucky.'

'Been living?'

'Pennsylvania.'

'A good, strong, free-swinging liar is one of the things that I like best in the whole world,' O'Rourke countered.

'You wouldn't mean to point that word at me, would you?' asked Pete, rather sadly.

'How far West you ever been?' asked O'Rourke.

'I went once clean back to Saint Louis,' answered Pete.

'Brother,' O'Rourke cautioned, 'they don't

cross their feet the way you do, lifting the foot up high, this side of the cow country. Why don't you try to be a little more reasonable?'

Pete looked at O'Rourke with a shake of the head. 'Now,' he said, 'I took you for an understanding sort of a cuss, but I see you're plain stubborn, and that's a shame. It ain't every man that can tell the age of a horse by the size of his teeth. Maybe you're like that.'

'Brother,' said O'Rourke, 'I've seen that you're a tough bird. But I aim to soften you up a little. McGuire, go bring in those pictures we saw, eh?'

McGuire left the room.

'Nice, big, trusting kind of a kid, ain't he?' said Pete with a warm voice. 'A kid like that will go a long ways in the world, I guess.'

O'Rourke merely grinned at him. From Pete's face his glance swerved suddenly toward the windows of the room. All were shuttered; all were curtained. He drew a small breath of comfort from the fact. McGuire returned with the seven pictures from the cloth-faced doors of John Cobb's dressing room. They were ranged under Pete's eyes.

The older man asked: 'Leave me have a filling of that pipe, will you?'

'Fill up the pipe for him, McGuire,' O'Rourke ordered.

'Why d'you baby him?' demanded McGuire fiercely.

'I'm not babying him, brother. Give him a

92

smoke. Sometimes it helps to clear the eyes.'

So the pipe was filled, placed in Pete's mouth, and lighted. He nodded a bright-eyed thanks toward O'Rourke.

'Lemme see,' said O'Rourke. 'Which of these fellows do you know ... outside of yourself?'

'Am I in that lot?' murmured Pete around the stem of his pipe. 'Why, so I am, sure enough. That's a kind of a good picture, too.'

'Where was it taken?' asked O'Rourke.

'Back of the barn down on the place in Pennsylvania,' said Pete. 'I recollect that the sun was mighty bright and ...'

'Let that slide,' said O'Rourke. 'Know any of the rest?'

'I gotta look,' answered Pete and began to study the pictures intently, one by one. At last he lifted his head to say: 'Don't remember a single soul of the lot.'

'Except yourself and Charles Latimer?' snapped O'Rourke with a sudden fierceness.

'Latimer? You got me all wrong, partner,' Pete objected with a melting frankness of voice.

'Why d'you go on trying to make a damned fool out of me?' asked O'Rourke.

Pete peered at him brightly. '*I'd* be the fool if I tried to make one out of you,' he said with a air of confession. 'I never thought that fat men run to brains until I seen you. But you've showed plenty tonight.'

'What were you after, here in the house?' questioned O'Rourke.

'I told you, partner. I told you just how it happened.'

'Just how it happened that you picked out a house where your picture was hanging big as life? You think that makes sense?'

'No, it don't make sense. Don't seem to make sense,' drawled Pete, as though he wondered mightily over the problem.

'Are you gonna break loose and talk?' asked O'Rourke. 'Don't you see that we got you cold? We know what share Latimer had. We know what share you've got. But if you make the job easy for us by coming clean, we'll give you a break.'

'Come clean about what?' queried Pete curiously.

'You won't talk?'

'Talk about what? I'll talk all night, if I just got a lead.'

'Listen! Latimer got into the stateroom where Cobb was riding. Slipped him the chloroform. Passed him out the window. You go on from there.'

'John Cobb? Who's he?' Pete feinted. He pulled earnestly on his pipe and watched O'Rourke with the open eyes of a child.

O'Rourke spat into the fire. 'Freshen that up, Mac, will you?' he asked, pointing to the burning wood.

94

While McGuire was employed, O'Rourke took the heavy iron poker and with the remainder of the twine lashed it firmly between Pete's legs so that they thrust straight out. Afterwards, he pulled off the prisoner's shoes and socks.

'Take the chair on that side and we'll edge it up till his feet are getting warmed up,' O'Rourke ordered.

'You mean you're gonna do it?' asked McGuire with round, horrified eyes.

'Why wouldn't I do it to a damned, low-down, sneaking murderer?' growled O'Rourke. 'There ain't any reason, is there?'

'He didn't murder me,' said McGuire. 'He could've bashed my head in, and he didn't.'

'It would've taken time and made a big noise,' answered O'Rourke. 'That's the only reason he didn't take you out of the pack. Do what I say.'

'I hate it like . . . .,' muttered McGuire, but he handled his side of the chair deftly as they pulled it up until Pete's feet were almost in the blaze.

'Wait a minute,' O'Rourke called.

McGuire instantly stepped back from the chair, breathing heavily.

'I'm gonna just start at the soles of the feet first,' O'Rourke explained to Pete, 'but I'll burn off your legs to the ankles, and be damned to you, unless you talk. Are you gonna loosen up?'

Pete's voice was perfectly calm. He said: 'Partner, there ain't hardly a man that I'd rather sit and yarn with than you. I like a man that knows something. I like a man that even only *thinks* he knows something. But, dog-gone me, if I could tell about things that I don't even think I know.'

'You fool!' shouted O'Rourke. 'What about the picture that was hanging in there? What about the far West that's written all over you? D'you think that you can blindfold me by lying?'

'I'm mighty sorry,' said Pete. 'I guess I couldn't explain things any too well.'

'Well,' said O'Rourke, 'we'll go ahead, McGuire!'

'All right,' McGuire agreed.

Pete's face began to shine. Not a muscle of it was tensed, and his eyes remained as placid, his brow as clear as ever; but a close, thick sweat was running down into the furrows of his cheeks.

'Right into the fire!' commanded O'Rourke, staring at Pete.

The pipe tilted up between Pete's teeth, and a small cloud of smoke jetted up from the bowl, but he said nothing.

'All right! All right!' said O'Rourke. He stepped back to the fire and scowled into Pete's face. 'Yeah,' said O'Rourke, 'murder, or anything. But I can't smack 'em down when they got nerve like you, Pete. I can't smack 'em down. Except for that I'd amount to something in the department. You'd read about me in the papers. But just because I'm so kind hearted and weak . . . it's the Irish in me, or something. I'm no good at all at the third degree!'

'Wait,' whispered McGuire. He held up a hand that silenced the detective.

'D'you hear?' murmured McGuire.

There had been a touch of wonder in O'Rourke's face at first, but now the sound grew perfectly audible. It needed merely the slightest attention to make out the long, steady, hushing noise made by the thin rushing of a draught under one of the doors. Another door or window at the back of the house must have been opened at that moment.

The hushing whistle ceased. Had someone entered, or had someone left?

CHAPTER TWELVE

Outsmarted

O'Rourke as he listened—as he grew tense— did a very odd thing indeed. He drew a cigar out of the breast pocket of his vest and lighted it, all the while his face still as a windless pool with thought. Automatic action hardly could go farther than this. When he had gathered the cigar into a corner of his wide mouth, he whispered out of the other side: 'McGuire, take the bedroom door . . . and have that gun along with you. I'll go back through the kitchen.'

McGuire nodded, the heavy automatic gripped tightly in his hand. He stuck out his jaw and went tiptoe, stretching out his left hand before him as though he were feeling his way through the dark. O'Rourke was almost at the pantry door when a voice yelled out, a sudden shout from Pete that exploded in the Irishman's brain like a bomb: 'Look out, Champ!'

O'Rourke turned his face and his gun for a deadly instant toward his prisoner. Then he shouted: 'At 'em, McGuire!' and tore the door open.

He ran through the pantry into the kitchen, shimmering like a clean white dish. A small panel door at the end of the room was open on a dim flight of steps that ran narrowly down into the cellar.

He stood at the door, listening. There was not a sound of movement beneath. Another door crashed open. It was McGuire, thundering in from the bedroom. His face stretched into a rubber mask of gray at the first glimpse of O'Rourke. He stopped short.

'If he's down there, he's out the garage door and away,' panted McGuire. 'I . . . nearly put a bullet into you, seeing you sudden like that.'

'Shut up,' murmured O'Rourke.

The wind, which had risen a little, hummed mournfully around the windows, a little, dolorous tremor of sound. Otherwise they heard nothing. He had come in through the rear door—the intruder—crossed the kitchen, opened the cellar door which O'Rourke had overlooked, and disappeared.

O'Rourke scanned the floor of the room and made out small moist spots of irregular shapes where somebody had walked from the wet of the grass outside across the room. Those spots went to the cellar door and then past it, so far as he could make out. He tried the top step of the cellar stairs with his foot, and the wood creaked noisily. It was hardly likely that anyone could have run down those stairs in haste without being heard.

'He's in the house,' muttered O'Rourke into McGuire's ear. 'He's still in the house. That way . . . back in the bedroom maybe.'

'Not a soul,' hissed McGuire.

'Look in the dressing room closets?' asked O'Rourke.

'No,' McGuire admitted.

'We'll look there,' countered O'Rourke and led the way. But before they had opened a single closet door, he spotted the place. Those small damp spots which he had traced across the kitchen proceeded more visibly across the rug of the dressing room, angled in toward one of the closet doors, and came out again from it, leading on toward the farther side of the room.

'Back to Pete,' whispered O'Rourke. 'If we've been fooled . . .!'

He plunged back on the run and snatched open the door to the library-living room.

It was quite empty. A few little twists of cut twine lay on the floor near the chair where Pete had been confined, but that was all that remained to remind O'Rourke of his prisoner.

The Irishman, running on like a wild bull, passed the fireplace where the flames were tossing up their arms in a little red dance of jubilation and on into the hall. He skidded into the door he was trying to open, cursed as he tugged it wide, and plunged out into the open.

Something thudded against the wall behind him. He heard the hard crack of an exploding gun. He knew that death had whipped past his face, and the sting of a raindrop against his forehead as he jumped sidewise from the light that issued from the door touched O'Rourke like the point of a sharp knife. McGuire, issuing from the same doorway, swerved to the detective's side and dropped to a knee, prodding the muzzle of the automatic forward in small jabs, so great was his eagerness.

There was only the wind in their faces, and the rain which came down in sudden volleyings. O'Rourke said at last: 'They're gone. No use blundering on through the dark and playing into their hands. They've got all the cards now, and we're the suckers!'

He went back inside the house. McGuire, following, closed the door and passed into the library where he found O'Rourke slumped forward in a chair, staring at the fire. The Irishman's face looked soggy and weak with age. As he seemed now, so would he be really in fifteen years. The clock had been turned ahead.

McGuire said gently: 'The other one ... he sort of sneaked into the closet there in the dressing room. I went by him like a damned fool. It was all my fault, not yours.'

'Shut up,' said O'Rourke. He took a champ at his dead cigar. His eyes were as dead as his smoke.

McGuire went back into the kitchen, picked up a bottle of Scotch and two glasses, and brought the cargo back beside the fire. He poured out two stiff hookers and placed one at the hand of O'Rourke. The detective made a tentative gesture and then shook his head a little.

'It was my fault,' said McGuire. 'I might've seen something, if I hadn't gone on blundering so fast. I'm mighty sorry, Mister O'Rourke.'

'Be still, will you?' muttered O'Rourke.

An instinct kept young McGuire talking. He went on: 'Then the fellow sneaks around in here, while you and me are in the kitchen. He takes and cuts the twine and sets Pete loose. The two of them heel it out of the house. We couldn't've missed them by more'n three jumps.'

O'Rourke said nothing. He was shrinking inside his clothes, turning into a pulp of weak flesh.

'Here,' commanded McGuire. He put the whiskey glass inside O'Rourke's hand. But the detective's fingers remained idle, lifeless.

'I didn't know I was hooked up with a soggy bum,' McGuire jibed. 'I thought I was workin' with a real man. Take a look at yourself. While you're winning, you look great, but when bad luck comes up toward the finish and looks you in the eye, you quit like a yella dog.'

O'Rourke stirred. He half rose from his chair and parted his lips to speak. Then he grinned, vaguely, around his cigar.

'You're right, brother,' he said. 'Yella dog is what I am.' He tossed off the drink, lighted his damp stump of a cigar. 'The race ain't over yet,' he nodded. 'The numbers ain't posted, eh?'

'Hell, no,' agreed McGuire.

'They took the pictures. Notice that?' said O'Rourke.

'Sure I noticed it,' answered McGuire. 'What else would I notice? They're on their way to beat all get out, but they stay long enough to pick up all of them seven big pictures. That means the pictures count. That means they're the lead to something big. They're the whole dad-burned show maybe.'

O'Rourke looked with new eyes on his companion.

'You're not a bad kind of a kid,' he said.

CHAPTER THIRTEEN

Twenty Minutes in Buffalo

Into the dingy station of Buffalo rolled the train from which John Cobb had disappeared. Rain streaked, it was like a long black thunderbolt going into a section of hollow gray cloud. It was seven-fifty as the air brakes brought the monster to slowness and then to a halt with a single swaying jar. At eight-ten the journey toward Chicago would be resumed.

Campbell, hollow-eyed with sleeplessness, had a telegram in his hands almost before the train stopped. It was from O'Rourke and read:

READ MORNING PAPERS AND SEE HOW COBB DIED STOP GOT A SUSPECT AND LET HIM GO STOP ALL SIGNS OF A BIG CREW WORKING THIS CASE STOP NOT A ONE-MAN JOB STOP LATIMER IS ONE OF THEM STEP WATCH HIM ALL THE TIME STOP
    REGARDS AND USE THE BEAN

Campbell crumpled the paper and stuffed it into his overcoat pocket. Then he changed his mind, lighted the yellow slip, and let it burn to a gray ash that dissolved in the air as it fell toward the floor.

103

'The poor Irish mug,' he thought. 'He needs me.'

Campbell laughed and sneered at the same moment. He prepared to get out and walk the platform.

*   *   *

Latimer, in his compartment, was already fully dressed. He had four hours of sleep under his belt and that was enough for him after he had yawned and stretched thoroughly. He was like a big cat as he roused himself and suddenly became wide awake, ready for the mouse hunt. He had himself shaved and dressed with the speed of a lad in boarding school, practiced in working against time, and he got out of his compartment with the taste of toothpaste in his mouth and the razor burn still tingling on his face. The weight of the gun under his coat comforted him more than money in his pocket.

Before the train slowed to a stop, he was at his post but only in time to see, from the platform, the door of Josephine Worth's compartment opening. The outside day, a muddy mixture of dawn and rain and station smoke, pushed hardly a ray inside the car. Only by the dim globes along the ceiling he marked her, covertly, as she passed on toward the opposite end of the Pullman and out on the farther platform. There were only twenty minutes to spend in Buffalo, and she seemed to intend to use them fully.

Then the train stopped. The doors opened. The stools were placed under the steps, and Latimer got down to the platform level. He was two seconds after the girl, two seconds before Campbell swung down from a rear platform. Of the detective Latimer remained unaware. His gaze was constantly before him on the hurrying figure of the girl. He had to swing into a good stride to maintain his distance behind her, swerving through the clumps of baggage, the scattering of passengers up and down the train, their faces studies in black and white under the station lights. The foul sweetness of sooty smoke remained in his lungs. He coughed to clear them.

The girl, walking as fast as she could, made straight for the gate. He could have recognized her, he told himself, by a single glimpse of her, no matter how she might be swathed in the gray fog of that tweed coat. She passed out from the station, and Latimer, well behind her, saw her hurrying almost at a run across the street.

He closed up on her, for even the struggling lights of the station were like full daylight compared with the murk of that smoking dawn with the streaking dimness of rain across it. He barely was able to distinguish her as she turned the corner. He was almost too late to spot the apartment house entrance where she disappeared. It was one of those narrow monstrosities on small lots peculiar to American cities, a raw, flat brick wall scattered over with small windows and the zigzag of a fire escape etched against the back.

Big Latimer opened the front door. In the little vestibule before the inner door he made out the dim names and numbers of the apartments. But the girl was gone. He thought of running in after her then withdrew, his lips pinched into a line, and hurried back across the vacant lot adjoining until he had a good view of all the windows that glistened up the side of the building.

One of those toward the rear, on the fifth floor, flashed out a light that was curtained instantly. It might have been merely someone getting up. It might have been someone rising to answer Josephine Worth's ring at the door.

Latimer glanced at his watch. Seventeen minutes of train time still remained before the departure from Buffalo, an excellent proof of the speed with which the girl had moved. He ran to the rear of the apartment house. A drainpipe close to the place where the last length of the fire escape was drawn up gave him his means of mounting. With foot and hand he swarmed up like a sailor and reached the first platform. There he paused, in spite of hungry impatience, to unhook the iron ladder and let it down. The end dropped from his fingers and fell with a heavy bang against the

106

concrete pavement of the back yard. Latimer winced. But since small things were not to be considered, he went rapidly up the escape, keeping all his attention well before him and scorning to glance down and back. That was why he failed to see the figure that rounded the corner of the apartment house, looked up, and then drew back cautiously.

At the fifth floor he found a window opening onto the fire escape platform. The shade was drawn down inside. The window was firmly latched. He opened a pocket knife, passed the blade inside the upper sash, and probed. It was a very good latch—strong, new, and free from rust. Therefore, it gave presently under the sidewise pressure, turning neatly. He began to work up the window. It was not an inch open before he made out the murmur of voices, a man speaking and then the sweet, pure, childish note of Josephine Worth.

Childish . . .? he thought. *Pure?*

As he raised the sash gradually, the warm air of the room thrust the bottom of the shade out, with a rattle, through the gap. The voices in the next room ceased. He thought of turning to flee, but a man clambering down a fire escape was a helplessly poor creature, worse than a monkey up a tree when the hunter comes with his gun beneath. So he remained there, holding the bottom of the shade down firmly with his fingertips. The whole curtain turned suddenly golden bright as a light switched on in the room.

'No, there's nothing. Must have been in the room above,' said the voice of a man, big, deep, a little husky.

'Raise the shade,' suggested Josephine Worth.

'There's not enough daylight to be worth a damn,' he answered. 'Come back inside, I want you to tell me . . .'

Footfalls went off into dimness, carrying the voices with them. Latimer began to press the window gradually up, holding down the tremors of the draughty shade with one hand. Afterwards, he had to roll it up—tie it with its dangling length of cord—before he ventured a leg over the window sill and into the room. The open door of the next room gave him enough glimmers and reflections to enable him to spot the nature of this chamber. It was a cramped little kitchen. The gas stove glimmered here, the sink there, and yonder were the deep bellies of the laundry tubs.

Moving to the side he looked in on a dining-living room where Josephine Worth sat opposite as big a fellow as Latimer ever had seen—a huge stalwart whose dressing gown flowed over him like a draping over a statue of Hercules. He was thirty, perhaps, dark haired, very handsome, just a suggestion of softness in his jowls, but the jaw, the nose, the brow all cut in strong, clean lines. The two argued in subdued voices. She called him 'Jim,' extending her hands palm up in gestures of graceful appeal, while he stabbed a blunt forefinger into the air, insisting on his point. Half the words were lost to Latimer until Jim said: 'We've got enough here. We could go to court even.'

He pulled from a folder on the table a newspaper, time yellowed and split at the edge of the pages. 'We got it here,' said Jim.

'Court? Go to court?' repeated Josephine Worth. She began to laugh in an ugly way, not throwing back her head with mirth but keeping her eyes level on the face of Jim and letting the laughter flow out softly.

'Yeah, maybe I'm a fool,' Jim said.

'You're only a little silly,' said the girl. 'Do you know what you ought to do?'

'You tell me,' he answered.

She leaned forward across the table and began to speak so quietly that Latimer could hear hardly a word, though he crept a little closer to the door, straining his senses to listen. He got out of sight of them, near the door, but still her voice was so lowered that it was difficult to make out anything, except that there was a persuasive music in her speech.

Her words became suddenly clear: 'You have to. It's a duty. You have to, Jim.'

'I'm a dog if I do it,' said Jim. 'I can't.'

'Kiss me,' said the girl, 'and tell me that you will . . . Don't you love me a bit, Jimmy?'

'You know I do,' groaned Jim.

'You can trust me, can't you?' she pleaded.

'Trust you? How could any man in the world trust you?' answered Jim.

'What have I ever done to *you*?' she asked with a wealth of sorrow in her tone that made Latimer's upper lip curl.

'No, not to me. Say that I don't count,' went on Jim. 'But . . .'

'I have to go,' she said. 'I'll barely make the train. Tell me that you'll do it, Jimmy, dear. Kiss me, and tell me that you'll do it.'

A chair scraped on the floor. There was a pause. Latimer heard the kiss.

'I'll do it,' Jim agreed.

'Dear Jimmy. *Dear* old Jimmy!' the girl exclaimed. Then: 'I've got to run. Good bye . . . good bye, Jimmy. Please love me . . . trust me.'

Latimer ventured a glimpse around the edge of the door and saw her standing at the farther door of the room, drawing it open, her face turned up toward Jim with a look of perfect, smiling faith. Yet not perfect, either, for Latimer's critical survey seemed to tell him that she was reading and judging the face and the mind of Jim at the same moment that she seemed to adore him. Latimer's mouth pulled hard to one side, a twisting grimace.

She was gone through the door, with big Jim striding after her, closing the door behind him. The yellowed old newspaper remained on the table.

Latimer got to it in a stride, folding and

thrusting it into the pocket of his overcoat as he turned away. He scarcely had moved when the door opened again, suddenly pushed inward.

Latimer went right in at him. A smaller fellow or one less steady in the nerves would have yelled out, he knew, at the sudden apparition of a stranger in the room that had just been vacant. This big Jim hardly made a sound and threw up his great arms into a defensive position like a practiced boxer, a high guard after the modern style, with his body sloping well forward and a long left reaching at Latimer's head as he rushed. It was going to be a fight, and there was no time for a fight. The train would be pulling out in a minute or two. So, as that long left shot out, Latimer let it come and drove in a right-handed counter. Jim's fist banged home on the side of Latimer's head, an inch above the temple. It staggered him. It swung him with a shouldering thrust to the side and slammed him hard against the wall. But his own hand had met Jim's jawbone solidly. The huge fellow sank at the knees, his dressing gown ruffling out, his eyes dull.

Latimer, reeling, went in again. He had to finish this before the wits came back into Jim's eyes, even though his own brain was spinning like a top. He struck for the chin and beat his hand vainly against the rubbery, thick cushioning of muscles on the point of that great shoulder. He tried again, and Jim's stabbing left bumped his forehead like the knuckles of a walking beam and knocked him out of time and distance.

It was an automatic motion on Jim's part. The mist was still across his eyes, but the brain was beginning to work through the fog. His knees had stiffened. His powerful right hand swayed back and forth, getting in rhythm to strike.

There was the gun inside Latimer's coat. He remembered it now, but this was not the moment to use it, according to his singular code. He reached for Jim with a long left that was blocked neatly. He stepped in then, with his last bid—a far-reaching overhand right with a whip-snap at the finish of it like a stone flung from a sling. It got the point of Jim's chin. At the waist and the knees he buckled like a steel beam twisted by a powerful explosion. His mouth sagged open, closed again. The last relics of his will power were used to thrust him forward. As though he realized that the accuracy needed for punching was gone from him, he flung out both his great arms and lurched at Latimer. And if those vast hands secured a grip, Latimer knew that he was gone. Between the arms, like a gun shooting a breach, he struck hard and short. Jim's head tossed. Twice his hair flew up before he settled slowly, like a tree bent down by wind, at Latimer's feet.

Latimer paused for one quick breath to look down at the size of that ruin before he ran out through the door and down the zigzagging stairs to the street. The daylight was coming more strongly through the morning fog as he ran for the station. He saw the minute hand of the big clock on the face of it marking ten past eight. If he lost the train, he lost everything.

CHAPTER FOURTEEN

Yellowed Paper

Detective Angus Campbell, breathing hard—half stifling as he controlled the laboring of his lungs so that no eye might be able to tell how he had been running at full speed—rubbed a peephole in the fog of the train window and scanned the platform with an anxious curiosity. He had seen gracefully hurrying Josephine Worth regain the train just as it began to move. Now it was gathering impetus more rapidly, and still no Charles Latimer appeared. With the swift ease of power the engine was accelerating, the wheels beginning to click out their rapid, broken, galloping measure. Porters and station men on the platform were jerking away across the window before the big man appeared.

He ran so fast that his legs seemed to be

blown back behind him, streaming as in a wind. The high lift of his knees kept his overcoat skirts flying level. He reached the side of the train, turned, began sprinting with all his might. Angus Campbell studied not the running style but his face. It was perfectly calm. That habitual smile still remained about the mouth as the big fellow was swept away to the rear by the gathering speed of the train.

He would never make it. The difference between his rate of going and the smooth, arrowy speed of the train would have broken even the grasp of a monkey had it leaped for the guard rail.

'That's that,' said Campbell and settled back in his place.

He began to sift the men of crime he had known, throwing out all other classes and coming to those smiling fellows who appear every now and then—the smooth, easy men who drew suspicion rarely, and then only because they are a little too professionally plausible. Big Charles Latimer was of that stripe. How he tied into the crime in this case Campbell could nearly guess. The telegram from O'Rourke informed him that John Cobb was dead. O'Rourke had picked up enough information to want Latimer watched closely. No doubt Latimer had been working the train end of the rich man's kidnapping.

The Buffalo morning paper which lay unfolded on Campbell's knee carried news of the event, obviously inserted at the last moment, on the front page. The heading was:

TORTURE DEATH OF MILLIONAIRE
John Cobb Kidnapped from Train, Burned

There followed a brief story of the disappearance of John Cobb from the train, together with the tale of how his trail had been followed to the spot where he was found, a blackened, charred corpse. His watch was found there. A dentist, dragged from bed at midnight, had identified his work in the mouth of the unrecognizable corpse. It was John Cobb, beyond doubt, who sat dead, wired into an iron chair, a crime of such unspeakable ferocity and savagery that the annals of murder hardly could match it.

It was probably a vengeance case, according to Patrick O'Rourke, the celebrated New York detective who had made all the startling discoveries that, so far, revealed the criminal. It was, Mr. O'Rourke declared, one of the most dreadful and mysterious murders of which he had any knowledge. The brilliant Mr. O'Rourke stated that he would not leave the case until he had solved it, granted permission from his superiors to pursue his investigations.

At the end of the article appeared the description of a man commonly called 'Pete,' one withered with age but still alert and active, looking like a young man when viewed from behind, with a light and springing step. In fact, a man of sixty or over. Also wanted was a person named 'Champ,' described only by that name because he never had been seen.

Campbell, as he finished this article, half closed his eyes and inhaled one deep breath which tasted of misery. 'The brilliant Mr. O'Rourke,' 'the celebrated detective,' was again taking the headlines. Sitting a little straighter, Campbell gripped his jaws hard together. Let O'Rourke flourish in the public gaze for a time. The profound roots of this crime—the beginnings of it—would be discovered on the train that now was rushing on towards Chicago.

Here a big fellow came sauntering up the aisle past Campbell. It was Charles Latimer, walking with his easy, athletic stride. The lurch and lean of the train as it struck a curve at high speed neither staggered him nor made him pause. There was nothing to indicate that he had done anything extraordinary except the occasional slight lifting of his shoulders. For he, like Campbell, was controlling his breathing, and Campbell recognized the signs of it.

An elderly man, reeling with the unsteadiness of the train, came past Latimer, who stood a little to the side and slipped a hand into the overcoat pocket which was nearest to the man who passed him.

Campbell took note of that. He left his seat

and wandered slowly up through the corridor of the train, sliding past men and women who were on their way to the washrooms, all with that half-sick look that follows a night in a Pullman.

He saw Latimer enter his compartment. As Campbell loitered in the rear, the big fellow came out again, minus his overcoat, and walked on. He had hardly passed out of the car before Campbell was inside the compartment.

The damp overcoat hung from the bracket hook on the wall. Wet shoes were in a corner. Speed was the motto of this Charles Latimer, in spite of his bigness. At the thought of a cat of such a size, a slight chill ran up through Campbell's spinal marrow. He picked up the shoes and eyed them earnestly, putting them down again.

He had seen Josephine Worth leave the station with big Latimer behind her. He had thought, as he followed them, that they intended a meeting in secret. But presently it had become apparent that the man was trailing the woman. This, to Campbell, was something of a shock, for he had taken it for granted that the two of them were combined in whatever work went forward. The discovery that they had at least some breach in their interests had stimulated him, as a fine new scent of game would stimulate the brain of a trailing hound. So he had watched the girl enter the front of the apartment house. Then he had observed big Charles Latimer climbing the fire escape to the rear of the building. His careful eye had not failed to note the light that glinted on the side of the wall before Latimer began his climb, and that was why he had looked up a railroad detective when he returned, panting, to the station. He had given the address.

'The fifth floor, rear. Pass the word to one of the city detectives. I want to know what sort of people live there. Wire on the news to me the first stop this train makes,' Campbell had ordered.

As these ideas moved swiftly through Campbell's mind, he dipped his hand into that overcoat pocket which Latimer had guarded in passing the man on the aisle. All that Campbell touched was the dry, crisp rustling of paper. He pulled out a yellow old newssheet, and his heart leaped.

CHAPTER FIFTEEN

Names

Turned in his seat so that passers-by up and down the aisle could not look over his shoulder, Campbell held the old newspaper issue inside the *Buffalo Morning Journal* and read with care. It was dated January 3, 1902, *The Willoughby Messenger*, Willoughby City,

Nevada.

WATER GAINS ON BLACK DIAMOND was the leading headline, spilled in huge type across the front page. A four-column spread told how Mike Loftus and Steve Berry, the well-known owners of the Black Diamond Mine, had vainly installed in their shaft a powerful centrifugal steam pump to fight the water that was rising and threatening to drive the miners from their work. Already they were sinking rises to explore the less valuable fringes of the vein instead of deepening the shaft into bonanza.

The devil's own luck is hitting Mike and Steve, *wrote the reporter in a familiar vein*. They prospected for years before they joined the Willoughby rush and struck it rich. Now water is drowning out their claim, or will the pumps beat it? Nevada has a dry face as we all know, but dig deep enough, and she spits in the miner's face.

Good luck to you, Steve and Mike! We hope that the bad fortune which has hit you won't spread to other diggings. We hope that the Willoughby Lode won't turn into an under earth lake.

What it seems to us is that if the water in the mine could be pumped out fast enough it would not only clear the mine, but it also would be useful to irrigate some of the waste of the desert. We've been to

119

California, and we know how alfalfa will grow like a happy weed on blown sand, even if a little water is turned loose on it.

Campbell, finishing that article with care, could find nothing in it. But he went on with his quest hungrily. By the very presence of the newspaper he felt that the murder of John Cobb had been dignified by linking it in some manner, perhaps, with gold mining. He could remember, in his childhood, the name of the Willoughby Lode coming like the face of fortune into the newspapers out of the Wild West. What had happened to the Lode he could not remember. But a deep, quiet delight began to spread through the heart of Campbell. A dead man, burned in an iron chair, a beautiful girl, a strong man, a kidnapping, a time-worn newspaper, the infinite possibilities of hates and jealousies that might spring from mining disputes—all of these elements combined to make, for him, a perfect picture. It was rare for Campbell to be satisfied, but this was one of the few moments of his life when he could tell himself that he had chosen the only profession in the world that matched his talents and his tastes. He would not have been any place other than in this hard, plush seat. He would not have been occupied in any way other than with the *Willoughby Messenger* of January 3rd, 1902. Now he was stretching his hand across thirty-three years and dipping into the grab bag of the past. Something would come up in his grasp, he was certain.

Flanking the account of the rising water in the mine of unlucky Mike and Steve was the story of a killing.

TOWN MARSHAL WATKINS MURDERED BY GYPSY GRANT

Death, the grim harvester, *began the reporter in poetic vein*, has summoned Marshal Watkins to the Great Beyond. No more shall we see his brave eyes or hear his cheerful voice or feel the security which his courage spread over the town.

Here the poetic vein gave out and the story went on.

Gypsy Grant was the fellow who did it, and the place was down in Jeff Murphy's saloon. Gypsy is a pretty mean man with a gun, as everybody knows, but he was down in Jeff's place taking his liquor like a gentleman and everything going along smooth and easy when the marshal stepped into the place to take his morning eye wash. When the marshal saw Gypsy, he stopped short. He said: 'Is that you, Gip, you chicken-stealing hellion?'

Gypsy looked up and said: 'Why, hello, Watkins, I thought you was still dealing them off the bottom of the pack back in Kansas City.'

Nobody knows who seemed to go for a gun first, but anyway the Gypsy filled his hand before the marshal. That being the case, there's no need to tell what happened afterwards. The marshal put his bullet through the ceiling as he was falling on his face. Gypsy certainly drilled him clean.

Afterwards, Gypsy stood up and said: 'I guess we'd all better liquor, boys. I want to get your opinions, was that self-defense?'

It's a hard question to answer. The boys have met up in several places and talked it over, but they can't make up their minds. It's a sure thing that Watkins led off with the first card and that Gypsy took the trick. The only thing certain about it all is that Watkins finished up dead. The bullet went right between the eyes. A nice bit of shooting, Gypsy, no matter what comes of it in the long run.

These two major events filled the first page, except for some advertisements in boxes, such as the arrival of a brand new shipment of clothes for ladies and gents to be found at Isaac Wilder's Clothing Store, everything straight from New York, and the latest Paris fashions for the girls.

On the second page it was announced that Tucker Vincent had just arrived in town from

Tucson. In the bottom of the same column Nordell and Breen were opening a new saloon on the corner of McKinley Avenue and Second Street. A little farther on there was an account of a little brawl in Westover's Dance Hall.

The fun got fast and furious in Stan Westover's place last night, *said the cheerful reporter.* Rose and Myrtle began to look in the same direction, and the direction they looked in was towards a handsome young fellow called Charlie Something-or-other. They got to mixing a lot of drinks with their conversation, and finally Rose reached over and put a knife into Myrtle right under the collarbone. It looked like the finish for Myrtle, but she turned out to be a right handy left-handed gal, and she socked Rose with a bottle. Rose went down and took the count; except for the pile of hair on her head she would have had a cracked skull. Myrtle is in the hospital recuperating. The knife missed the lung, so there won't be anything but hard feelings when she gets out on the street again. Hit 'em first, Myrtle. They don't amount to much when they're lying on the floor.

On the third page, another noisy headline announced:

PETE WINSLOW STRIKES IT RICH

Where did you get it, Pete? *began the account.* The real stuff; loaded with a good silver background just to keep up the interest? Where did you get it?

We know the assay report. We know a whole lot about the ore. All we lack the knowledge of is where the claim is. As soon as we found out about it—we have a bird that whispers things like this—we went around and congratulated your partners, Pete. We went to Harry Champion and Dick Worth and Alexander Latimer, who looked bigger and handsomer than ever. We talked to Tom Waterson and Jay Markham and Milton Glenn. We congratulated them and we hoped that they might tip us just as much as a wink about the direction, even, in which the big claim lay. But they didn't wink at all. Most of them had too much whiskey even to open their eyes. And the rest just kept laughing all the time—not like darned fools, but like millionaires!

Well, good luck, boys. The more the merrier. This printer's devil doesn't envy the fortune of good fellows.

But what about the Gulch? What about Boulder Gulch? It wasn't there that you made the strike, was it?

This unusual article ended at this point. Only the patience of Campbell had caused him to read it through to the finish, but something about it made him begin to frown and run back over the words.

He had not completed this second survey when a hand gently and firmly pulled down the upper edge of his Buffalo newspaper. Another hand reached down and grasped the *Willoughby Messenger*. He looked up into the faintly smiling face of Charles Latimer, who was taking the old newspaper from him. The grip of the detective had relaxed with numbness to such a point that he could not resist.

He could only study the eyes of Latimer, now pale with light, and that frozen smile, as the big, young man said: 'That trail of a skunk is easy to follow, Campbell. If the eyes can't read the sign, the nose can smell the way, as a rule. But I hope you enjoyed the old print, eh?'

He stood over Campbell for a moment with that same faint smile and the pale, brilliant eyes, and Campbell had nothing to say. Even O'Rourke used to admit that it was impossible to silence the Scotchman, but now not a word came from him. A sort of darkness spun in his brain. He reached into it and never a word came to his tongue but, in a sort of chant, that list of names which he had read: 'Winslow, Worth, Champion, Latimer . . .' There his mind stopped, as Charles Latimer turned and went on casually down the aisle.

It seemed to Campbell that he had been, at

this moment, both a coward and a fool. Yet, as he listened to the train tapping out its volleys against the window pane, he felt that he had seized on a nugget of truth that might become enormously important later on in this case. Crime detection is not considered a pursuit essentially important or noble, and yet Campbell's soul was stirred with the same sort of selfless joy that floods the heart of the great astronomer when some new conception— some key to an explanation of the universe— fits into a mysterious question and opens a door, however small, through which he can peer out at the enormous origin of things. So Campbell felt, and yet without as yet arriving at the definite point which might cause him so much happiness.

As the geometer knows the solution of the problem in his mind while there still remains an interval during which he must concentrate on abstraction before he can place the problem and its solution on paper, so Campbell pondered what he had read in that last article.

There was not much. There was hardly so much as the floating feather which will tell how the wind is blowing, but his mind fastened on the fact and clung to it.

'Latimer.' That was the name which stood out of the list.

It could hardly be coincidence. Even if he had found that newspaper on the person of a Smith or a Jones, still the fact that a Smith or a

Jones had been mentioned prominently in the news would have been of the highest significance. But Latimer was not a common name. Four or five of them in the whole New York directory was all one would find. Therefore this became enormously important.

He wrote out a telegram to be sent off as soon as possible. Duffy, at headquarters, knew nearly everything in the world. If he did not know, he would find out. So Campbell scribbled:

SEND ALL INFORMATION ABOUT WILLOUGHBY LODE IN NEVADA PERIOD ABOUT 1902 STOP WIRE ME ON THIS TRAIN IN FULL DETAIL AND TRY TO CONNECT THE NAMES OF WINSLOW CHAMPION WORTH LATIMER WATERSON MARKHAM GLENN

It seemed a miracle that he could remember all seven of them. It proved that the moment his eye struck on those names a bell had rung in his brain and called his unconscious to attention.

CHAPTER SIXTEEN

Truce?

Latimer, in the lounge car, kept his body relaxed and his mind tense with watching Mr.

Angus Campbell in one corner of the car and Miss Josephine Worth in another. His need was to look straight before him, as though dreamily, and from the corners of his eyes study the strained, distorted images of the detective and the girl, because every change of their faces might convey some valuable information to him. It was a prolonged tension, but he was accustomed to endless strains and endured this with a steady grimness of purpose.

When the train roared into the next station, the newspapers came aboard first of all and then the Western Union boy, carrying his yellow envelopes. His snarling voice called in the lounge for Josephine Worth, Angus Campbell, Oliver Kilbane, Johnson McCarthy, Charles Latimer.

Latimer ripped open his own message and read:

ON THE JUMP BUT STILL RUNNING DRAWING ACCOUNT CANCELED

The signature was 'Biff.' He folded this, slid it into a pocket, changed his mind, tore it into small bits, and dropped it into the wastepaper basket beside the writing desk.

Far beyond his own time of reading, both the girl and Detective Campbell were perusing their own messages with a frowning intentness. Long messages, extending over more than a

128

single page and to be read and reread because the words in a telegram, no matter how expected, always come as a surprise and seem to contain interlined mysteries.

He bought a newspaper. The train pulled out from Detroit and slid on while, over the edges of the sheet, he watched the girl and the detective, with the same newspapers, busily putting their telegrams away at the same moment.

Latimer scanned the newspaper. The murder of John Cobb was reported far more at length than in the Buffalo sheet, for it appeared that Cobb had, for some time in his youth, lived in Detroit. As he read, Latimer smiled his usual smile but did not fail to note that the girl, from behind her own paper, was scanning him with deft side glances. Then she had risen and was leaving the car. It seemed to him that in the shadows at the end of the passage she had turned and flashed a single backward glance at him.

He hastened through the rest of the account. John Cobb's millions, said the newspaper, came largely from a lucky or clever find in the Willoughby Lode in Nevada. He retired rich. His investments had spread into many other fields. A peculiar feature of his life was that he had built for himself a little neat cabin of a house where he did all the work and refused to have a servant about him.

He got up and walked from the car and felt

the eyes of Campbell drilling into his back as he went past the detective. He continued straight to his compartment, paused at the door of it, and thrust the door suddenly open. Josephine Worth was just rising from her knees with that yellow old newspaper which he had placed with such care under the rear seat of the compartment.

As she faced him, she let the paper slip out of her fingers and drift back again to the floor. The wind of that mild descent caused the pages to spread out, rustling as they landed on the carpet.

Latimer locked the door behind him without taking his eyes from her. He saw the sudden movement of her hand toward her bag. Purposely he did not interfere and saw in her face the change of her mind.

'Wouldn't have been worth while, would it?' asked Latimer.

She said nothing, watching him. Some of the baby curves had been stricken out of her mouth. Her eyes were no longer languorous, childish. He noticed the deep, quick breathing.

'Sit down,' said Latimer.

She shook her head.

'You're staying for a while,' Latimer announced.

'I'm leaving now,' she answered.

'Sit down,' he commanded.

'Shall I have to ring for the porter?' she asked.

'Here's the bell,' offered Latimer.

She reached her hand instantly toward it, touched it, but did not press. Latimer laughed a little.

'Sit down,' he repeated.

She slipped onto the seat. She had one arm braced well out beside her as though to help her if she wished to spring up at any moment. He took the place beside her, which forced her to move her arm.

'Afraid?' he asked.

'I wanted to explain why I was in here,' she said.

'Go on and explain,' he suggested.

'No. It's no use,' she answered.

He picked up the fallen paper and folded it.

'Not on account of this?' he queried.

'Well . . .,' she began, but her voice ended there.

'Go ahead,' said Latimer.

'I saw you take it from Mister Campbell.'

'I'll bet you did,' he agreed.

'And so . . .,' she ended.

'And so what?'

'I suppose that we're here in the same sort of an interest, aren't we?' she asked.

'I don't give a damn about the interests,' answered Latimer's calm voice. 'Give me that bag.'

She gripped it suddenly with both hands.

'Give it to me,' directed Latimer.

'Ah . . .,' murmured the girl.

'Wishing you were a man?' he asked.

She looked him straight in the eye. Perhaps because of his bigness, perhaps because of the pale light that came into his own eyes at certain times, no one ever had met his glance like this, like a strong hand gripping another hand, holding it, struggling for the mastery. She stared straight into him, and he felt the cold shock and the wonder of it.

'Yes,' she said. 'I'd like to be a man for a moment or two.'

'And bigger?' he asked.

She said nothing. Quietly, devoutly, she was hating him with her look. He took the bag from her limp, gloved hands and opened it. It was one of those big affairs, of crocodile, brown, deep, capacious. In an upper compartment there was a compact, a wisp of a handkerchief, and another folded absurdly small. He took the fresh one out and sniffed at it.

Then he nodded. 'You have good taste,' he said. 'In brandies and perfumes and all that, I mean. How's your taste in men, Josephine?'

She felt no personal affront in this but continued to look at him with the same singular abstraction as though he were far beneath her ken, on a lower level of existence, a thing to be studied and remembered, like a beast safely behind bars. She gave him no answer but continued her cold survey.

Into the bottom of the bag he reached and

drew out a neat little automatic, short of barrel but not small of muzzle. At ten yards it would kill a man as well as any Colt forty-five, and it would spit out five bullets at once.

'Pretty,' he said. 'Compact and pretty ... like you, Jo, eh?'

He felt the cold of her silence, but merely laughed again.

'Damned beautiful and damned poisonous,' said Latimer. 'But I've been in tough spots before ... malaria swamps and all that. I rather like 'em. What I want is literature. Reading matter is what I crave, darling.' He pulled out a crumpled yellow twist of paper and read, as he pulled the telegram out straight:

DICK IS HELPLESSLY SINKING STRIKE NOW
TOM

'That's the one you got last night,' he said. 'Tell me about Dick?'

He looked into her silence, explored it, almost wondered over it.

'How does it feel to hate like this?' he asked. 'Better than wine, isn't it? Better than Rhine wine and soda on a cold day, eh? Tell me about it, Jo. How does it finger your heart? You have a heart, haven't you? Or what is it that makes the tremor there in your breast? Just a machine? How much human blood is there in your whole body, beautiful?'

She turned her head from him and looked

out the window. He scanned the line from brow to throat with a critical care and found it perfect. The daylight struck on the side of her neck and left a highlight glistening. By the look of her skin he could tell how it would feel to the touch. Like the thinnest panne velvet rubbed with the grain.

He felt into the purse and took out another telegram that ran over two pages. It read:

LOST MESSENGER IMMEDIATELY AFTER YOU WENT KNOCKED OUT FOLLOWED HIM TO STATION STOP LOOK FOR BIG FELLOW HANDSOME SMILING DIFFERENT EYES BROWN SUIT BE CAREFUL
JIM

'There's one word in there that I like,' said Latimer.

She turned her face toward him again. She was smiling suddenly. Her challenge had gone from her eyes all in a moment.

'Handsome,' she suggested. 'That's the nice word, isn't it, Charles?'

'How you turn it on and off,' said Latimer. 'How damned clever you really are, my dear. What a brain, what a brain.'

'You have a nice voice,' said the girl. 'When I close my eyes, like this ... Now say something, Charles.'

He said: 'When you look dead, like that, I could imagine you in stone and all the boys falling in love with your face when they go to the museum on Sunday afternoon.'

'That's it,' she answered, without a smile, opening her eyes. 'When I don't see you and just listen to your voice, it warms me, Charles. It makes me want to say: "Charlie, why shouldn't we throw in together and work for the same end?"'

'When you say that to yourself, what's the answer?' asked Latimer.

'Why, then I see you,' said the girl, 'and I watch your smile, and I realize that I'm just a silly little romantic fool.'

'Ah,' said Latimer. 'When you talk like that, I almost love you, Jo. When you talk like that, all chisel edge and brain and no blood in you, nothing human, I almost love you.'

'As you'd love a pretty little mummy,' she suggested.

'How did you guess that?'

'You're not tremendously hard to see through,' she said. 'There's the surface polish that almost blinds the eyes, but the rest is glass, and one can see through it . . . rather foggily, to be sure.'

'I'll keep the telegram for you,' he said.

'I thought you would,' she answered.

'But I won't keep the gun,' he went on and handed it to her, butt first.

A white devil touched her face as she felt the gun in her hand. The bright of her eyes fell like a frost on him.

135

'Well . . .,' she said and reluctantly put the gun back into the bag.

'Between you and me,' he said, 'how close was that?'

'How close was that?' she asked.

'How close to murder?'

'Oh, not very,' said Josephine.

'Take it by and large,' he said, 'I imagine that you still owe me something.'

'For what?'

'Why, for the gun. It's a new gun, and it would kill five men like nobody's business, wouldn't it?'

'Yes, if I could shoot straight enough.'

'You could shoot straight enough, couldn't you?'

'Perhaps I could,' she answered.

'No matter what a ratty little crook you are,' he said, 'I think you realize that there are obligations that ought to be met. You ought to pay me for that gun, don't you think?'

'Well?' she asked, thoughtful and curious about him.

'Just a touch of friendliness perhaps?' he said. 'What about it?'

'Certainly,' she said and tilted back her head a little.

He leaned over her. 'Ready?'

She pursed her lips a trifle.

'All ready,' she said.

After a moment she looked out the window again.

136

'I knew you wouldn't,' she said.

'How did you know?' asked Latimer.

'I'm really a very gifted girl,' she said.

CHAPTER SEVENTEEN

Pot Shot

When the train reached Jackson, newspapers and telegrams came aboard at once, the telegrams first. In the distribution Angus Campbell received three of the open-faced yellow envelopes. Two of them were in fact for him, but the third was addressed to that fellow with the black eyebrows and the red mouth, Grosvenor.

Campbell ruthlessly opened it and read:

MEET YOU CLIFTON CHICAGO WITH FIRST INSTALLMENT

The signature was: 'Partner.' The place of sending was the town of Lassiter, Minnesota.

'Here,' Campbell called to the lounge car waiter. 'This was given to me by mistake. Know anybody called Grosvenor?'

'That gentleman right back there,' said the waiter. 'Thank you, sir.'

He took the opened telegram back to the end of the car where Grosvenor was just rising from his chair to stretch his legs on the platform. At the same time a pair of riveters, at work on new building or repair work in the station, opened up with a frightful roar.

Grosvenor, receiving the telegram, scanned it and then looked sharply towards Campbell, and Campbell, from the corner of his eye, was aware of that half startled, fixed, angry surveillance. He said to himself, as he opened his own message: 'Rotten. Something rotten about Grosvenor. In stateroom . . . rotten.'

Something rotten about Grosvenor, something odd about the fear that had been in Grosvenor's face when he realized that a detective had opened his telegram. A detective must weave suspicions as fragile as spider threads until he has made a net strong enough to catch a tiger. Campbell felt a sudden tugging along his nerves, as though prey already were caught in the net.

He bought a newspaper, tucked it under his arm, and went on with his telegrams. The tall, stalking form of Grosvenor passed down the aisle before him, eyes fixed upon a proud future, disdaining the littleness of ordinary men.

The first wire was from Buffalo, reading:

PARTY HAS WEEKLY LEASE HAS OCCUPIED FIVE DAYS NAME CHESTER PARKINSON HABITS REGULAR DRINKS LITTLE OTHERWISE UNKNOWN HERE

The alias preyed heavily on Campbell's mind as he turned to his second and longer telegram from New York. It read:

WILLOUGHBY LODE LOCATED BY STEPHEN WILLOUGHBY 1902 ENDANGERED BY RISING WATERS IN SHAFTS 1903 GENERALLY ABANDONED 1904 AND 1905 SURFACE VEIN DISCOVERED AND WORKED IN 1932 BY JOHN COBB MILLIONS TAKEN FROM GROUND IN ONE YEAR STOP YOUR NAMES UNTRACEABLE SO FAR EXCEPT FOR PETER WINSLOW CONVICTED MURDER 1903 GIVEN LIFE PARDONED 1932

The 'Peter' before that name of Winslow knocked at the door of the detective's mind. Peter it had been, he could swear, in the list which he had seen in the stolen copy of the *Willoughby Messenger*. Another link, freshly forged in the chain, grappled a new and perhaps important fact to the list which Campbell was compiling.

His mind scattered through his evidence. Grosvenor, Josephine Worth, big Charles Latimer—all in the stateroom of Cobb before the kidnapping and murder of the millionaire. The adventure of Latimer and the girl in Buffalo. The warning from O'Rourke about Latimer. The guilty face of Grosvenor when he read the telegram that had been opened. The intimacy of Latimer and the girl, and yet the fact that he had obviously spied on her in Buffalo. And always the knowledge that in the background of this case were fifteen millions of dollars—even if they were largely newspaper dollars. It seemed to Campbell that the clues enriched him more than gold. Mentally he was rubbing his hands as he stood up from his chair. He sauntered down the aisle to take his turn on the platform, the newspaper still under his arm.

In the list of the old names, including a Latimer, there had been the Winslow first of all, the fellow who had made the rich strike and then gone to prison for murder—to prison for life. With Winslow as partners were Latimer, Worth, and all the rest.

Campbell, reaching the end of the car at this moment, rested a hand against the wall and took a breath. Worth was the name of the girl, Josephine Worth. She must represent one of the seven. Chance does not appear in such forms. Coincidence never occurs in groups and clusters of events.

Descending to the platform, he shook open the newspaper. The uproar of the two riveters was joined now by another pair, turning the wide hollow of the station into a frightful bedlam which drilled gradually through the ears and deeply into the brain. Campbell forgot the racket as he glanced over the repeated story of the murder of John Cobb. It was a long and detailed manuscript by this time and, above all, there was a new edition in the form of a considerable story about the presumptive heir, Lawrence Pelton, whom the press representative had just interviewed.

The article ran:

From the desolation of the Minnesota wheat fields to the presumptive possession of fifteen million dollars is the happy fate of Lawrence Purvis Pelton who, when informed by this correspondent of the death of his cousin, was struck dumb. When told the terrible details of the death he closed his eyes and after a moment was able to say: 'If it costs the entire fortune, I'll run them to ground!'

In a smooth field near the house stood his powerful airplane, an amphibian with which he was tinkering when the party arrived, one of us an airplane mechanic from the flying field near Lassiter . . .

Here the mind of Campbell paused, and he took careful note. Lassiter . . . from that town Grosvenor's partner had sent the telegram. Campbell swallowed a grin of joy and read on:

. . . from the flying field near Lassiter, bringing with him a broken part of the motor whose absence had kept the owner out of the air for several days. The newly rich man, suffering from a burn across the mouth caused by lighting a cigarette when his mustache was moistened with grease and gasoline from working on the engine, looked like a poor mechanic. He has been on the farm for over a year, and the airplane is the last symbol of the fortune which has slipped through his hands.

Campbell recalled the wizened ferret of a John Cobb whom he and O'Rourke had taken under their protection for the trip to Chicago. That this fellow could have been loved either by woman or man was too absurd.

Campbell grinned inwardly while the thundering and cataracting uproar from the riveters burst upon his brain. He had gone from the track a little past the end of the train. Now he turned and sauntered back. He was nearly opposite the first coupling, at the end of the lounge car, when the hat was jerked from his head.

A wind scurried it rapidly before him, so that he had to run in pursuit. When he picked it up, he stood for a moment stiff, staring. He looked up and scanned the windows. Yonder a few people were leaning out, talking, waving to acquaintances along the platform.

Someone was calling out: 'All aboard!' The last farewells shrilled thin and distant through the thundering of the riveters. Still Campbell stood in his place examining a double hole which had been cut through the top of his hat.

It was of the dimension of a forty-five caliber slug.

The train had begun to roll away before Campbell came to himself and ran after it.

CHAPTER EIGHTEEN

Too Many Clues

Even before the train reached Buffalo, Patrick O'Rourke was pacing the living room floor in the house of John Cobb while McGuire sat half asleep by the fire. The shades still were down, and the daylight merely served to make them visible. Rain fell in thin whispers and smashing volleys while the wind talked to itself far away or came yelling in the ear of the house.

'Why couldn't Cobb keep servants, Mac?' asked O'Rourke, waking the other.

'Why won't a mean dog keep company with another pup? Because it thinks every other dog is like itself . . . ready to bite.'

'You mean that Cobb was afraid of other people, eh?'

'Sure. When he went down the street . . . and that wasn't often . . . he looked at the face of everybody that was far away from him. He kept his eyes squinted, studying every mug that came along.'

143

'Why did Pete and Champ come back here to the house?' queried O'Rourke.

'They wanted the seven pictures,' said McGuire. 'That's what they wanted, and when they got 'em, they cleared out.'

'They didn't want the pictures . . . not first of all,' O'Rourke objected. 'Look here.'

He went to the davenport and pointed out half a dozen small holes in the tapestry covering, mere needle holes.

'Probes,' said O'Rourke. 'They been probing the furniture to find something small. And come in here.'

He led the way into the dressing room and opened one of the doors. He pointed to a shelf on which handkerchiefs were piled on the one side all socks on the other.

'The piles ain't very neat,' said McGuire.

'Was Cobb neat?'

'Yeah, he sure was. You mean that somebody else stacked up those things?'

'We found Pete in the cellar,' said O'Rourke, 'but that's not where he'd been spending his time. He'd been going through this place with a fine-tooth comb, putting everything back but not putting it back quite right. Look at the shirts on the shelf below, too. And here's the rod with the suits hanging. See those two pockets turned inside out? Something small was what Pete was looking for. The question is . . . will he come back?'

'He won't come back,' said McGuire. He

144

pulled up a shade. Through the wet dimness of the morning half a dozen figures were visible snooping across the lawn through the trees. 'He won't come back,' he repeated. 'I knew that half the town would be up here looking things over. Murder gets people worked up. Like buried bones get a dog excited. They'll be walking around, everywhere.'

'Maybe you're right,' said O'Rourke. 'I dunno. Pete is about the toughest that I ever seen. I've got to go out. Can I leave you here alone?'

'Sure,' said McGuire.

'You already been rapped once,' answered O'Rourke.

'That's why I won't be rapped again,' replied McGuire.

'All right. You stay on here and keep your gun handy.'

*   *   *

The backtrail to which O'Rourke directed himself lay right up through the trees to the summer house where Cobb's body had been found. On the way he marked a dozen rain-coated figures. At the summer alcove itself two or three score were gathered silently, staring motionlessly at the fire-stained chair in which the dead man had sat.

When O'Rourke appeared, a murmur went through the spectators. They turned to him.

The water dripped steadily from the brims of their hats as they stared at the man of the law. O'Rourke waved to them cheerfully.

'Found anything for me, boys?'

They all shook their heads at him, brilliancies of water flinging past their faces. They were pleased by the familiar address of the 'great detective' but they had found nothing.

He picked up a handful of the sand through which he had trampled the night before. A dense circle gathered around him and watched with bending heads and peering eyes.

'Any of you know where sand like this could be fetched from?' he asked.

'Yeah. The bank of the river,' said someone.

'It's more white than the river sand,' said another.

'Back by Peekskill you get sand like that,' said another.

O'Rourke, sifting the sand from one palm to the other, noted a little black pebble. He dug his thumb into it. The outer blackness came away under the edge of his nail and revealed the gray glint of the true stone beneath. There was tar or thick oil about, wherever that pebble had been lying. O'Rourke headed towards the railroad.

Behind him the crowd fanned out in a moving mob that remained a dozen paces behind at the nearest. He took the backtrail up which he had come the night before. The daylight at its worst was better than the torchlight by which he had examined the ground in the first place. The grass, nourished by the freshness of the rain, had sprung up straight again almost everywhere. But in a flat, naked bit of clay surface he found a single footprint lightly embedded, the sharpness of the edges a little dimmed and rounded by the downpour.

Beside it O'Rourke squatted on his heels and, after a moment, he took out his tracery of the shoe of John Cobb, for this mark was also small for a man and large for a woman. The tracery corresponded perfectly. He would not believe it at first. John Cobb had been chloroformed and passed through the window of the stateroom. His body then had been dragged brutally up the slope.

That was the story which he had to believe, but here was a fairly good proof that John Cobb had not been dragged at all, but that he had walked over the ground. What was the weight then that had been pulled over the grass so carelessly? Was it John Cobb that had stepped here, or was it a man wearing the shoes of Cobb?

There was not much doubt about the print. The smallness of it spoke loudly. Besides, there was the angle of the front edge of the heel, and the hand-fitted curve of the forward sole. It was most surely the footprint of Cobb's shoe.

O'Rourke, rising, lighted a cigar and cursed

softly, gently, thoughtfully. He went on, still in his thought, toward the railroad. His brain was spinning. When he had slipped through the railroad fence, he looked up and down the side of the track with a grimly expectant eye until a small, light-colored patch was noted. To it he went at once. It was sand, of the exact quality which he had found at the summer alcove. And in it, here and there, were little pebbles. Streaks of old oil were sprayed into the sand. Some of the pebbles had turned black with it. Moreover, the loosely compacted surface of the ground had been scooped away here, as though a quantity of the sand had been carried away. A small pool of rainwater was filling the hollow.

CHAPTER NINETEEN

O'Rourke Cements a Friendship

O'Rourke, savagely chewing the end of his cigar, tried to fit the new suggestions into the old picture. John Cobb, when the train stops, recovers from the fumes of chloroform, finds that he is missing whatever the thieves took while the chloroform was operating upon him—and, instead of sending for his double bodyguard to inform them of what has happened, he uses the emergency alarm, stops the train, climbs through the window, and drops to the ground.

O'Rourke grunted. It was the sort of a theory that made him blush, for he thought of the corrugated-iron face of Corrigan were his own voice to suggest such a theory.

He continued the logical train of events as that footprint and that scooped place in the sand suggested it to him. John Cobb, having left the train, skulked behind one of the piles of ties until the train passed on. He then took off his coat—or some bag which he had prepared for the purpose and, bending in the rain without shelter from the wind and the wet—his overcoat had been left on the overland—he proceeded to scoop up the sand until he had placed a considerable weight in the coat—or bag—which he then proceeded to drag up the hillside in order to lay a trail to the spot where he sat in an iron chair and waited for himself to be burned alive . . .?

Even omitting the last step, the whole theory stunk to heaven in the nostrils of logical Patrick O'Rourke. It was nonsense which he could not possibly offer to Corrigan. It was nonsense which he could not present to a far greater man than Corrigan—one Patrick O'Rourke, first-grade detective. He was left, in fact, with no theory at all.

He trudged back up the hillside through the woods, struggling with the problem, and remembering what Corrigan was always saying:

'The thing that ain't possible is the thing that links up everything.'

Usually he preferred, when analyzing a crime, to put himself in the criminal's boots and to walk backwards to the crime. This mental gale made the earthly one through which he was passing a thing of no moment, though the trees were bending to the storm and pale billows of wind and rain marked the grass and dimmed the air with their passing.

Coming to the house, he went into a darkened living room. The fire had burned down. McGuire was not there.

'Hey, Mac,' called O'Rourke.

His voice had no echo. It dropped away into a murderous outburst of the storm which jumped close to the little house and shook it with both hands in a fury.

'Ah, well, damn it,' muttered O'Rourke. He thought somewhat yearningly of Campbell, that adroit, astute, wakeful man who habitually was at the point where he was most needed.

'McGuire! Hey, McGuire!' shouted O'Rourke and, through a breathing space in the uproar of the storm, he heard the echoes of his voice fly thronging through the house.

He started back through the kitchen and pantry. The pure white of the kitchen was clean as a bowl. He pushed open the door of the dressing room—and shut it suddenly, softly behind him. For McGuire lay in a corner on his back with blood on his face.

He had one arm across his breast, the other thrown straight out, as though he were wigwagging, or doing a bit of semaphore. A dark, red, glimmering pool spread out around the middle of his body.

'They done you in, kid,' said O'Rourke. 'The dirty devils . . . they done you in.'

He took out a new cigar and lighted it, spitting the bit from the end far away across the floor. He took off his hat at the last moment and sloshed it down, a loose rag. Then he kneeled. He pushed his hand under the edge of the lad's coat over the heart. The heart was pumping away steadily, strongly.

He saw what had happened after that. There was a streak of red on the corner of the mop board where McGuire's head had struck. The blood on McGuire's face came merely from a shallow scalp wound—granted that there were no fracture beneath. But a far more serious injury was the source of the blood which had soaked into the rug and pooled upon the surface of it. A bullet had entered the front of the thigh of the right leg and issued behind through the buttock. He lifted McGuire's knee. The bone was not broken.

O'Rourke almost laughed in the greatness of his relief. He picked up his wet hat and pulled it down over his eyes. Then he dragged off McGuire's trousers and began to make a bandage with strips of sheet from the bed. The lad stirred, groaned, gripped at the air with

151

both hands.

'I'm gonna bash your head in . . .!' growled McGuire. 'Hey, O'Rourke,' he added, 'I thought that Pete . . .!'

'You're gonna be all right,' said O'Rourke soothingly. 'Lay back and take it easy. It was Pete, wasn't it?'

McGuire braced his shoulders and bleeding head against the wall.

He said: 'I heard something, just a light bump. I come in here. All I seen, when I opened the door, was those shoes. Before I lifted my eyes, a gun went bang. I saw Pete and another fellow jump for the kitchen door. I tried to follow them. My leg wouldn't work. I dropped and whanged something, and it went black.'

'All right,' said O'Rourke. 'Am I hurting you much, kid?'

'No, it's okay,' McGuire answered. 'Think of that dirty Pete, will you?'

'What else would I be thinking about?' demanded O'Rourke.

He was looking sidewise at the shoes. He had not noticed them at first. Now he saw a line of them topsy-turvy, lying outside an open door of the dressing room shelves. Within, other pairs remained.

Another strip of the sheet, torn into a narrower portion, he wrapped around McGuire's head. 'How is it, Mac?' he asked.

'Fine as silk,' nodded McGuire, twisting a grin onto his pale face.

'You're a good plucked one,' O'Rourke commented. 'Mac, I like you fine.'

'That goes double,' replied McGuire.

O'Rourke went to the back door and opened it. Now that the storm had lulled a little, the lurking watchers were coming out from the edge of the woods again to draw a little nearer to the dead man's house. He waved a pair of them to him.

'You got a car around, boys?' he asked.

They had one. Would they take a wounded fellow to his home in the next town? Their eyes were starting out in a happy excitement and pride. It would be a banner day in their lives, of course.

When they had loaded McGuire into the rear of the automobile, sitting aslant to ease the tortured leg, O'Rourke leaned inside.

'Would you like to come to the big town and work with me?'

'Me? I say yes,' McGuire breathed.

Their hands closed together. 'I'll be seeing you,' said O'Rourke.

'You bet,' answered McGuire. 'So long.'

'So long, kid.'

O'Rourke stood back and watched the car start. A side stroke of the wind made him stumble and nearly lifted the wet hat from his head. He was damp all over, damp to the skin, against which his clothes stuck, but his heart was light as he watched the car swerve out of sight down the drive. It seemed to O'Rourke that

153

he himself was again young, at the beginning of things. It almost seemed to him, for the brief moment, that his hands once more were clean.

CHAPTER TWENTY

Old Friends

In the house again O'Rourke roused the fire to a good, strong, companionable blaze. After that he went back into the dressing room to pick up the search where it had been left off.

The section of shelves which now was open contained several rows of shoes. Pete had been working right across. The shoes which had been moved had not yet been replaced but lay scattered on the floor, the hollow aluminum trees removed and the paper with which the trees were lined in the shoes torn to expose the bright metal beneath. The missing object must be very small and flat, if it could be pasted in under the sheathing of paper.

The remaining shoes he took out one by one, tapped the heels and soles to sound any hollow places, removed the aluminum trees, and tore out the paper linings. He had out the fourth or fifth of these and was about to put down the trees when he noticed that that metal under the paper did not show its usual clean face. Instead, there was a blur which, when he

154

turned the tree to the light, proved to be yellowish paper, a thin sheet of it, slightly wrinkled by the manner in which it had been fitted to the curve of the aluminum.

He had the rest of the outer blotting paper off in a moment and easily detached that inner fold of paper. The moment it was open in his hand, he knew that he had what Pete and Champ had been searching for so industriously. Perhaps it was for the sake of the design that John Cobb had been wired into the chair. Perhaps because he would not reveal the place where the mystery was hidden, he had been burned to death by the tormentors.

The bit of paper was perhaps five by seven. One edge was rough as though it had been attached to a writing pad. The quality was cheap. It was hardly better than a school copy pad, and it had been folded twice across so long that, as he opened it, the paper cracked and threatened to break off into four sections.

What O'Rourke saw was a very simple design with figures written along the sides of the lines in the following manner:

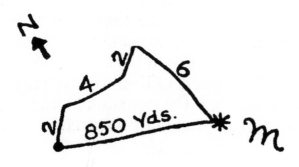

The longer O'Rourke stared at the thing, the more his heart fell. This design, so invaluable to Pete—so worth murder itself—had to him hardly any meaning. The 2, 4, 2, 6 no doubt meant hundreds of yards. The clumsily sprawling 'M' at the side had no meaning at all, so far as he could see. Given the key point or any point on this design, it was plain that one of the locations, either that marked by the heavy dot or that signaled by the star perhaps, must be a spot of the greatest importance. Here was a treasure, in short, which no man could use unless he possessed along with it some additional information. He needed a key point over which this design could be superimposed.

The telephone rang with a sudden and terrible loudness. His heart jumped. It was a moment before he could force himself back into the pantry and take down the instrument.

'Hello! Hello!' he called.

'Mister O'Rourke?' called a strongly nasal voice.

'That's me,' he answered.

'We just thought we'd ring you up,' whined the voice, 'because Officer Willisen and another state trooper have just picked up the man you want and another fellow that was along with him. We've sent out a car to take 'em to you. Is that right?'

'Right?' shouted O'Rourke. 'What could be wrong about it? Of course it's right! I'll be waiting. Get the name of the second man? Is it

Champ something or other?'

'He ain't a talkin' kind,' said the voice. 'Maybe you can get something out of him but not us.'

O'Rourke hung up and went back to the living room. He poured himself a good hooker of whiskey and spilled it down his throat. That lonely fear which had been standing like a ghost behind him now vanished away, leaving him feeling like himself again.

He heard the rush of automobile tires a moment later and got to the door in time to see a big sedan draw up. One trooper was inside it in the back seat. Into the front seat beside the driver had been squeezed Pete and his companion. A second trooper followed on his motorcycle.

O'Rourke, on the threshold, rubbed his hands cheerfully, like a host welcoming guests at an inn. He called out and waved to them as Pete and his companion got from the car, their wrists handcuffed together.

'Good work, boys,' called O'Rourke. 'Where'd you get 'em, eh?'

The trooper on the motorcycle swerved his machine to a stop at the side of the entrance and dismounted.

'Found 'em heading up the old quarry road. There's nothing at the end of that road. Nobody would be traveling it.'

'I'm proud to know you,' said O'Rourke. 'I'm mighty proud. Come inside here and have a drink. How are you, Pete? You wouldn't know how glad I am to see you. Hello, Champ.'

'Hello, O'Rourke,' said the companion of Pete and then suddenly pressed his lips together.

'That's all right,' said O'Rourke. 'I would have known that that was your name, because you've got the looks of a champion, is what you've got. Come on in and sit by the fire.'

Champ was of an age with Pete but so much fuller in flesh that he looked a good bit younger. When he came into the house and took off his hat, he exposed a rosy, bald head without a hair on it, except at the base of the skull. That head of his was built high behind and sloped all the way down to the eyes. Except for the wrinkles in it, it was hard to define and bound the limits of the forehead. He had twinkling eyes unshadowed by eyelashes, a blunt bit of nose stuck in the middle of things, and a wide, cheerfully smiling mouth. He was not tall, but he was built massively from foot to shoulder, and his skin was weathered to such a brown as only long days at sea can give, as a rule. He had a husky, bubbling voice, as though he had just been eating greasy food. His bright cheer was that of one who makes the best of everything.

'Did you show these fellows to McGuire?' asked O'Rourke of Willisen.

The trooper nodded. 'He recognized 'em,' he said.

O'Rourke said: 'You boys step out there

into the kitchen and find yourselves something to drink. Sit down, Pete. You and Champ take these chairs over there. Good to see you again, Pete.'

Pete answered as the other three moved on into the kitchen: 'Why, it's like old times, O'Rourke, ain't it? It ain't the years you've known a man, it's the things you've done with him that counts, ain't it?'

'That's right,' said O'Rourke.

Willisen paused at the doorway.

'You gonna be comfortable, all right, alone with the two of 'em?' he asked.

O'Rourke nodded at the tall young man. 'I'm gonna be right at home with 'em,' he said.

CHAPTER TWENTY-ONE

Equal Shares

The door closed behind Willisen. Mild sounds of celebration began to issue from the kitchen, voices bursting out in laughter and ending in sudden silence.

'When you come to think about it,' said Pete in his pleasant way, 'it was hard luck that *we* had, wasn't it? How could we know that the damned road only went to a quarry that wasn't a quarry no more? Who'd think of keeping up a road as slick as a baby's cheek when it didn't go no place any more?'

'It *was* mean luck,' agreed O'Rourke. 'How much did you figure on getting for shooting down young McGuire?'

'I dunno what you mean,' answered Pete.

'You wouldn't know, would you? I guess it was Champ that did it?'

'Champ, did you do it?' asked Pete, turning to his companion with concern in his face.

'Put a slug into a fine young fellow like that?' echoed Champ. 'What sort of people does O'Rourke think we are?'

'Just boys out on a vacation,' said O'Rourke. 'That's all I think you are. Just a pair of fine, high-spirited kids.'

'Now you get the idea,' agreed Champ and grinned.

'You didn't have your eye fixed on nothing like this, did you?' asked O'Rourke. He took out his wallet with slow precision, shifted his cigar across his mouth to the opposite corner with a powerful waving contortion of the lips, and jerked a puff of smoke toward the ceiling. Afterwards he drew out the old fold of paper. The other two sat bolt upright, staring fixedly.

'Belong to you?' asked O'Rourke.

Champ had flushed a brilliant red. Pete was gray. They devoured the paper with their eyes.

'Now listen to me, you mugs,' said O'Rourke, dropping his voice. 'You know what comes to you for this job?'

'We're gonna be retired to an old people's home, I guess,' said Pete.

'More'n likely you'll take a trip up Salt Creek,' said O'Rourke.

'What's that mean?' asked Champ.

'The chair, you fool,' said Pete.

'I dunno,' explained O'Rourke, 'maybe it would turn out all right, and you'd only get twenty years for burglary and felonious assault. But maybe somebody would get mean. Cobb murdered like that, and then the pair of you breaking into his house to search for what he wouldn't tell you about. Maybe a jury would take and believe that you fellows did the killing. What you think, Pete?'

He said: 'Yeah, you're right. They'll give us the chair.'

'Now suppose we take and look at it from my angle,' said O'Rourke. 'How young do I look to you?'

'You look like whiskey could still make a boy out of you,' suggested Champ, and he smiled in the most friendly fashion.

'I look that way, do I?' muttered O'Rourke.

Champ leaned forward. O'Rourke's gun jumped into his hand, and he snorted out a cloud of cigar smoke.

'Don't make those quick moves,' said O'Rourke. 'I know the pair of you are regular chums, but I walked in my sleep one night when I was a kid, and I've been nervous ever since.'

He pushed the old fold of paper forward.

'You draw the design inside of this, Pete?' he asked.

'I ain't an artist,' said Pete.

O'Rourke said: 'Now, suppose this job meant something big, how much would I be declared in?'

They stared at him then at one another. Speech seemed to be qualifying the brightness of their eyes, so perfect was their mutual understanding.

At last Pete glanced back at O'Rourke. He said softly: 'Equal shares, O'Rourke.'

'Shares of what?' asked O'Rourke.

They looked at one another again. Again there was that silent semblance of interchanging speech. Then Pete said: 'Three or four million in an outcropping vein of ore.'

'It ain't ore,' Champ said. 'It's just rock with the gold soaked into it. Call it a vein if you want to. I'd call it a wing of the government mint.'

'I come in equal partner, do I?' asked O'Rourke.

'We make an even split,' declared Pete.

For an instant real temptation gripped O'Rourke. It went through his brain like a sweet poison. He had to look down at the muzzle of his gun and breathe out a cloud of smoke.

He was still looking down when a hand, withered and lean, gripped the barrel of the Colt and jerked it out of his grasp. That was Pete. Another hand, which came from

Champion, caught him by the coat lapels and pulled him suddenly forward. A blow smashed his head down against the table.

*   *   *

It seemed to O'Rourke that a jingling of small bells was sounding like Christmas on the margin of his mind. Afterwards he was aware of pain that filled his head.

A voice was yelling: 'Yes, sedan. Number is 1408. Got it? Two of 'em. Send the alarm. You're got their descriptions. Put it on the radio. Hurry it. O'Rourke is maybe murdered . . .'

O'Rourke opened his eyes and raised a hand to the excruciating pain in his head. He felt the warm moisture of blood.

'Good for you,' said Willisen, standing by. 'How you feeling?'

O'Rourke got to his feet.

'They smashed me and ran,' said O'Rourke, staggering towards the door.

'I shouldn't have left you alone with the two of them.'

'Sure you shouldn't,' groaned O'Rourke. 'You should have seen that I was a fat-headed old fool. Fat in the brain. A soggy, worthless old fool.'

163

CHAPTER TWENTY-TWO

Escape by Air

The air was alive, reaching after the two fugitives with electric fingers, touching traces of them here and there. O'Rourke, with a plaster hastily stuck across his wounded head, gripped hard the armrest in the back seat of the radio car that was tearing fast on the road to Manhattan. The reports came through loudly.

The sedan had stopped at a small shop twenty miles down the river, and the blacksmith had been forced to smash the locks of the handcuffs to liberate the hands of the two criminals. They had taken his rented car, leaving their stolen sedan. They were on their way now in a small convertible.

A little later the convertible was found up the mouth of a narrow lane. Where were they now?

They were near New York before the radio bawled out fresh news. The two had been pursued by a motor cop for speeding and, one of them, reaching coolly out through the window of the car, had put a bullet through a tire of the motorcycle. The policeman had turned in the alarm.

O'Rourke's machine swept on, its siren

164

screeching as it overrode the traffic lights and turned the red to green. Another report. A little closed car near Jamaica had been sighted and, in it, two men who resembled the fugitives.

'They're way away from us,' said the driver of the car.

'Stop the car,' said O'Rourke.

The driver pulled up.

'What would they be doing on Long Island?' said O'Rourke.

'They got a hide-out there, maybe,' said the policeman behind the wheel.

'Hide-out? Pete's too smart to trust anything to a hide-out. Pete ... he'd aim for a take-off place.'

'Well, an airplane, then?' suggested the man behind the wheel.

'Get me to a phone,' answered O'Rourke. 'You've got it, boy.'

A short time later he was calling: 'Corrigan! Is that you, Corrigan? O'Rourke. Watch every airport around. Watch Long Island fields. They're going to be in the air before long. Will you spread the word? What comes from Campbell?'

'Campbell's gone crazy,' Corrigan replied. 'He wires for the history of a mine out West.'

O'Rourke roared: 'If he wants to know that, he's not crazy. What mine?'

'The Willoughby Lode. Out in Nevada. He wanted to know about some names.'

'What names?'

'Here they are . . . Winslow, Champion . . .'

'Did you say Champion? Short that to Champ, and it's the man we want. What other names?'

'Worth, Latimer, Waterson . . .'

'Corrigan! There's a Latimer on the train with Campbell . . . and a Josephine Worth!'

'Markham and Glenn are the last two. They happen to mean anything?'

'I don't know. Everything means something. Count those names, will you?'

'There are seven of them.'

O'Rourke yelled: 'Then I've seen the seven faces that go with the names.' He panted: 'Campbell? What else did he want to know?'

'We looked up those names. Couldn't find anything about anybody except a Peter Winslow.'

'A *what* Winslow?'

'Peter Winslow.'

'Is that my old pal Pete? What about him?'

'Nineteen Oh Three. Murder. There in Nevada. He got life. Pardoned couple of years back.'

'It's him!' cried O'Rourke. 'I knew that there was murder in that scrawny mug of his. I'll ring you back for news. Will you step on it, Corrigan?'

The radio car took O'Rourke farther out, across Brooklyn, into the open country. He was free from the city when he stopped at a filling station and telephoned back to Corrigan in New York again.

The voice of the inspector came roaring down the wire.

'We've got 'em, O'Rourke, and we'll put 'em in the pocket,' called Corrigan.

'Where were they spotted?'

'Your tip did the work. They've taken off for Chicago. We bag them there.'

'Is there a fast plane for Chicago?'

'Wait a minute. I'll let you know.' A moment later the voice of Corrigan came over the wire: 'You can get a plane in fifteen minutes. I've made the reservation for you. Go fast. Here's the address . . .'

'Find out about that man Winslow murdered out there thirty years ago and more,' O'Rourke requested. 'Will you find out? Everything! Find out everything . . .! I've got to run.'

CHAPTER TWENTY-THREE

Warning

The huge monoplane carried only a dozen passengers from New York towards Chicago—three women and nine men. It was the first passage for one of the ladies. She was a squat little Jewess, wrapped like a bale in her fur coat. When the plane began to go over some of those airy bumps that sink the heart into the stomach or lift it into the throat, she closed her eyes, sank back in her seat, and gripped the paper bag close to her chin for hour on hour.

Two or three of the others were made from time to time a little apprehensive by the bucking of the great plane and looked at one another with startled eyes. But on the whole the trip was smooth enough. The big ship had been so newly and so strongly insulated against noise that the roar of the motors sounded no more, say, than four riveters on a steel building a block away. The radio could be heard and, in fact, was heard to the indignation of a tired old man who continually was aroused from sleep by some crackling outburst of static.

In pauses of the radio the stewardess, all crisp as snow in her uniform, was monopolized by a red-faced, elderly fellow in a rear seat. He kept his big hands crossed in his lap and looked up with a sidewise grin at her. She was willing to talk. It was the first airplane she had been in that permitted any conversation quieter than shouting in the ear.

'This is a great dodge, isn't it?' she asked.

'Yeah,' he said, 'it's the only noise we ask for that means the right thing.'

He took off his hat and ran his hand back over a completely bald head, except for a moderate fringe at the rear. She noted with a sort of amused sympathy the high back of his head and the continual slope down to the eyes, the forehead etched in with a modicum of wrinkles.

'Yeah,' he said, understanding her glance, 'it sure makes a difference when the hair is lifted off your head. A lot of dog-gone popular braves, in the old days, must've gotten unpopular after their scalps was lifted. What you think?'

'Well, it's cool,' laughed the stewardess.

'It makes a whole lot of face to wash,' he replied. 'This is a dead quiet ship, ain't it?'

'You can talk. That's the big difference,' she said. 'I used to land all bottled up, and I didn't care who would listen.'

'How long to Chicago now?' he asked.

The plane mounted over a heavy bank of clouds, golden or white with sun on the upper surface and deepening to dark seas beneath.

The girl said: 'Half an hour. A little less. We're making good time.'

'How you come to get into this line of work?' he asked.

'Boy friend of mine got a job as a pilot. That was what made me air minded, as they say.'

'Ever cruise on the same plane with him?'

'No, he broke off with me as soon as I got fixed in an air job.'

'What kind of a bozo would that be?' the man asked.

'Art was all right,' she answered, cocking her head in thought. 'He just said that I was already too dizzy, and that after a couple of tail-spins I'd have to be put in a can and kept cool for ten years before I got back to normal.'

'A mean bird, eh?'

'No, Art wasn't mean. He was just kind of a deep thinker. He knew I didn't have much brains.'

'You got a lot of brains,' said the bald-headed man. 'Anyway, why would anybody wanta carry around a load of fat in the head? It wears out the legs.'

'Anyway, Art up and left me. Good old Art.'

'Gonna marry him one of these days?'

'Maybe. I've been married twice already.'

'Get out! You? You're not twenty-two.'

'Marriage is only a sort of a quickie, these days,' she said.

'What happened to those marriages?'

'One of them got boiled and bumped into a truck. It was a terrible mess. The other marriage got to Reno. Reno's a swell place. Ever been there?'

'I've been there,' he answered. 'I've been there when it was only a sand lot.'

'People are kind of different there,' she said. 'They know how to have a good time. They don't keep *thinking*.'

'Yeah, that spoils a party,' he said.

'Don't it?' she confided. 'I hate a nine-o'clocker.'

'What's that?'

'One of these fellows that has to get to the office at nine in the morning. They start getting a conscience about midnight.'

'I never thought about that. That must be

hard on a girl.'

'It's terrible,' she said. 'Fellows like that are only human on Saturday evenings, and Saturday is always so crowded everywhere that's worth going to ... The news is coming on.'

The crooning which had been issuing from the radio stopped and a brisk voice began: 'Good evening, folks. This is the news from WRFZ. WRFZ speaking. Weather colder tonight ...'

'Weather,' murmured the girl. 'As though weather made news!'

'Well, I've seen rain in the desert,' the bald man remarked. 'That kind of weather can make a difference.'

'Oh, the Cobb case,' said the girl and was all ears.

'The murderers of John Cobb have been located, it is believed,' said the announcer. 'They are thought to be one Peter Winslow and a man named Champion. They are still at large. Please pay attention! They are still at large and perhaps are now in the air on their way to Chicago.'

A man in a front seat suddenly sat up a little straighter.

'They are thought to have taken a plane from Long Island for Chicago,' went on the voice. 'Their description is as follows: Peter Winslow about fifty-eight years old. Withered face but looks young in the distance. Expression smiling. Height about five ten, weight a hundred and fifty. Gray hair. Light step. Makes a good impression. Champion about the same age, height five feet nine, weight a hundred and eighty, still very strong, expression pleasant.'

'Think of a murderer looking pleasant,' said the girl.

'Yeah, think of that.'

'Champion,' said the voice, 'is almost completely bald. Head high behind, not much forehead, short nose, wide mouth . . .'

The stewardess looked down, agape.

'Steady,' the bald man cautioned. 'What's the matter?'

She was too benumbed with fear to move anything except her lungs and her vocal chords. She tilted back her head and began to scream. Every soul in the plane except the fat Jewess leaped up.

'It's him! It's him!' she yelled.

Champion stood up with a gun. His big voice boomed through the cabin: 'Sit down, ladies and gentlemen. Nobody is gonna be touched. Nobody but brash fools. Just set down and take everything easy, will you?'

They sat down, slowly. One of the women began to cry into her hands. The men looked thoughtfully at one another; each gathering a slight frown of resolution, as though he were considering violent action in this emergency. From a forward seat a gray-headed, slight fellow pushed open the door to the pilot's forward compartment and climbed up into it.

He stood in the blackness, in the volleying

172

roar of the engines.

'Down!' he yelled at the ear of the pilot.

The man turned his head, frowned, and then saw the gun.

'Down! And somewhere short of Chicago!' yelled the passenger.

The assistant pilot began to turn slowly in his place. His chief motioned him to be quiet. The big machine began to wheel slowly around and around in the air.

In front of them they could see the smudge of the great city, a dark pool that kept spreading out toward the horizon. Underneath, the woodlands were brown and gray patches. Houses were so small that five of them could have been put on the five tips of the fingers. The ship was like Gulliver in Lilliput.

As it wheeled on down, everything seemed pouring up to meet it. The hills became defined. The trees separated one from another. At last they could see the glimmering windows that took the western sun and see the glaze of ice here and there across the great meadow toward which the pilot was aiming his forced landing. So imperceptibly were they settling that they seemed to be standing still until the wheels touched the ground, and suddenly they were a part of the earthly world that shot back around them at a dizzy speed.

CHAPTER TWENTY-FOUR

Reunion

The Chicago papers came on board the train only a quarter of an hour before it reached the station. Campbell got one and found the Cobb murder spilled large on the front page. There were two features of importance. One was a last-minute box in heavy type that read:

ARE COBB MURDERERS IN AIR FOR CHICAGO?

And under it: Two men about sixty years old, suspected of the murder of John Cobb. Their names are Peter Winslow and Champion.

'Peter Winslow ... Harry Champion ...,' muttered Campbell, remembering the list of names.

The second new feature of the Cobb story was a photograph of the dead man. It took his lean face, with its hollow cheeks, from a favorable angle. He looked much younger than his years, and the neat, short-trimmed mustache gave a foreign air of spruceness to his features. It was a good copy of the original portrait and even showed clearly, in the lower corner, the words: 'To my friend Jerry Hill, from John Cobb.'

Campbell took out the envelope in his pocket on which was written down the fate of fifteen million dollars in a staggering handwriting. The signature was exactly like that on the picture.

The writing of the body of the will was different. The motion of the train would explain, of course, a good many of the jerks and the uncertainties of the script, but it was necessary to recall the craven terror of the writer to understand the continued irregularities. When he came to the signature, he had done well enough. Campbell's own signature as witness and that of O'Rourke also were turned out with hardly a flaw. No, the motion of the train could not have explained all of these jerks and waverings. To be sure of it, he took out his pen, turned the envelope to the address side, and commenced to write. There had been little more motion then than there was now, and yet he was managing a fairly clear bit of writing.

He was thoughtful when he put away the envelope and the pen as the train slowed gently for the last stop. There was not much for him to find suspicious. There was no more, say, than a drop of ink to stain a whole quart of water, and yet a little shadow, a tiny filament of doubt had entered the Scotchman's brain.

He picked up his bag and descended to the

platform, keeping his eyes well before him where the towering head and the great shoulders of Latimer wadded through the crowd. His attention was so fixed in advance that he was startled as if by a gunshot when a husky, deep voice said: 'Hello, old mother of vinegar.'

'O'Rourke!' cried Campbell.

'What put you on the Willoughby Lode?' snapped O'Rourke.

'Come on,' said Campbell. 'I want to keep an eye on some of these fellows ... that Latimer ... remember?'

'Yes, but the Willoughby Lode?'

'This whole job is tied into the Willoughby Lode, one way or other. Cobb made the money out there. Listen. There are seven names ...'

'In the dressing room at Cobb's place there are seven pictures. I've seen the seven faces,' said O'Rourke.

'The devil!'

'What the hell of it?' demanded O'Rourke, suddenly rejoicing. 'Yes, or seven devils,' he added.

'Have they got Winslow and Champion?' asked Campbell.

'Listen ... hear the kids yelling the story?'

A voice sharp and thin and high as a rooster crowing was yelling: 'Cobb murderers force airplane down! All about the Cobb murderers!'

O'Rourke said: 'They forced a landing. The fool radio warned them. Where the two of them are now, nobody can guess.'

'If the whole gang is working together,' said Campbell, 'Latimer might lead us to 'em.'

'I'll tail him, Angus. Who do you take?'

'I wish there were three parts of me,' said Campbell. 'I'd follow the girl, and I'd follow Mister Grosvenor, too. I'll have to take him.'

They had passed on through the station. The murk of the evening lay heavily over Chicago. The blind, dead, cold autumn of the year had come. Winter, in comparison, is cheerful. The white of its face makes one think straightforward to the cheerful spring, but in the autumn there is only the wet, dripping sense of the death of the year.

'Where do I keep in touch with you?' asked O'Rourke. 'If we're gonna scatter out like this, we've got to know where to find each other.'

'Ring me at the Clifton and leave a message for a Mister James Angus.'

CHAPTER TWENTY-FIVE

Setting a Stage

The Clifton Hotel is all marble, glitter, noise, and immensity. New York hotels are mild mannered in comparison. The flow of guests for dinner, dancing, and the huge bar is even greater perhaps than the current of those who actually have the expensive rooms of the place.

Campbell checked his bag at the luggage room, went into the bar, and took a Scotch neat, in small sips. He was in no hurry, for he had seen a small, dark-faced man with the white of tape across his upper lip. That would be Lawrence Purvis Pelton, he was reasonably sure, who leaned over the card of registry and wrote. Grosvenor, after entering the place, had disappeared before Campbell could spot him, but there was no haste if Pelton had a room in the hotel.

The warmth of the bar soothed Campbell. Each moment he felt the long vibration of the train easing out of his body, leaving his brain also. The Scotch pleased him to his very nerve centers. When he had finished it, he went to the mail clerk.

'If messages come in for James Angus, please take them,' he said. 'I'll be registering for the night, I think.'

After that he went to the room telephone and asked for the room number of Mr. Lawrence Purvis Pelton.

'No Pelton registered,' was the answer.

'Maybe not,' agreed Campbell. 'Try Purvis. Lawrence Purvis?'

'Seventeen oh nine,' said the operator. 'Shall I connect you?'

178

'Not now,' said Campbell.

He went to a corner of the great lobby and waited with that hungry patience which had devoured him for so many years of his life. At last he saw Grosvenor come out of the elevator, looking taller, more magnificent than ever, with Lawrence Purvis Pelton stepping rapidly beside that stately stride. They turned into the entrance of the dining room.

Campbell, following as far as the great arched entrance, saw the pair take a corner table at the farther end of the big room. He returned to the desk and asked for the key to 1709. It was given without question, and a moment later he was unlocking the door.

It was a single room furnished in greens and yellows. Rather a small chamber and rubbed a little dingy already in its short year of life. Grosvenor, he saw, had stood in front of the fake fireplace. Three big gray dabs of cigar ashes littered the floor there. They reminded him of the stateroom on the train. Signs of footfalls went up and down, slight darknesses in the nap of the deep, gray rug. This, then, was where little Mr. Pelton had hurried back and forth.

It had not been an amicable meeting. Mr. Pelton had walked up and down, the sign showed, and occasionally had made sudden darts at Grosvenor to make a point.

A pigskin bag lay in the corner. Campbell opened it and went through the contents.

There was nothing in the slightest degree suspicious about the contents of that case. He went to the desk in the corner and examined the white blotter upon it. Even when he squinted from the side, he could make out no more than a few vague impressions. He took out a pencil with a broad, soft lead and commenced to shade the blotter, making strokes so light that an almost imperceptible layer of gray was transferred to the paper.

He had started at the center and worked outwards. He was almost at the lower right hand corner before he found what he had hoped for. Not a single word except the signature, but even this pleased him a little. It was very dim. The impression was so very light that he barely was able to make it out. He took from his pocket a slip of very thin, transparent celluloid, and onto this he traced the signature with the utmost care, moving the pen as though he were incising a design in metal. He had the letters at last, not trembling and uncertain as most tracings are, but running with a bolt, free movement: *Lawrence P. Pelton*. That bit of celluloid he returned to his wallet and left the room.

On the whole the trip had been not disappointing. He had learned to his own satisfaction that Pelton and Grosvenor, in spite of that signature of 'Partner,' were not friendly. And certainly the hired murderer could hardly be on amicable terms with the man who paid him.

The elevator slid down to the first floor with a breathless whisper. He walked out into the echoing noise, the marble brilliance of the lobby, and returned the key to 1709. The clerk, remembering him, gave him the usual swift, mechanical smile and nod of recognition. All clerks are fools, mused Angus Campbell.

He passed slowly across the entrance to the dining room and marked his pair in the distance, Pelton listening with a frown, Grosvenor talking with large and formal gestures, including a large sector of the room like an actor to a public audience. Campbell went to the desk and asked for one of the hotel detectives. A fat man, wrinkled from the chin to the eyes with queer cross lineations, was instantly beside him.

'I'm Angus Campbell, from New York,' Campbell began.

'I know about you, Campbell,' the hotel detective answered.

'You do?'

'I remember you and O'Rourke ... that poison case in the house on the island ... I read it, Campbell. Tell me, what can I do?'

'There's a man called Grosvenor in the dining room. Wait till he finishes dinner. Then take him somewhere so that you can go through him. You'll get a gun on him, I think. You'll also get a wad of hard cash. Put me somewhere to listen to what he says. Can you do that?'

The detective scratched his chin. 'We're here to protect the guests, not to bother 'em,' he said plaintively.

'Brother,' said Campbell, borrowing O'Rourke's usual word, 'I think Grosvenor has bothered one of your guests, all right. I think he's bothered him for several thousand bucks. And if he has . . . it's murder.'

'Murder?' murmured the house detective. He licked the fat of his lips. 'Come along with me,' he said.

He took Campbell to a small office which opened from a hall behind the lobby. An inner door opened into a larger room with a counter across it, as though to make a bar for the handling of questions. 'Suppose we keep this door open a bit?' he suggested.

'What's your name?' asked Campbell.

'Burman.'

'Burman, when you get Grosvenor, handle him with gloves. Mind you, I think he's a good shot, and I'm pretty sure that he has a gun. Take another one of the boys along with you. Will you do that?'

'Sure,' said Burman. 'If you've ever been burned, you're glad to wear gloves.'

'Now, mind you. If you find that he has a gun, and if you find that he has a wad of new money on him, you're to say one thing to him. Will you remember?'

A frown of anxiety came to Burman. 'You tell me. I'll try to get it,' he said.

'Say this . . . "Does murder pay that well?" You have that?'

'I have that,' answered Burman.

'Say just that. "Does murder pay that well?"'

'All right. And then?'

'Then give him back the money. Give him back the gun. Let him go.'

'What?'

'I mean it. Give the stuff back to him and let him go.'

Burman began to sweat. 'If he thinks that I haven't got anything on him, he'll complain to the manager.'

'Complain? With an unlicensed gun on him! Complain?'

'Sure, sure! The gun . . . if he's got a gun, it's all right. But you want to turn him loose?'

'I do. The main thing for you is to watch his face. If you find the money and the gun on him, watch his face when you speak your line about murder. Will you do that?'

'Like a hawk.'

'I'll wait in here. Go get him when you can,' said Campbell.

'What murder is it?'

'One murder's as bad as another,' said Campbell. 'Go ahead and do your stuff.'

CHAPTER TWENTY-SIX

Conference by Duress

The door of that inner room Campbell kept ajar the least fraction of an inch, just so that his eyes, placed behind the crack, would command a considerable wedge of the smaller office. He could see half of a map of Manhattan and its environs on the wall and part of a brown, varnished desk. He knew, even as he stood there, that he would remember this slice of existence as long as he lived.

A moment later Burman and another fellow brought in Aloysius Grosvenor. Campbell almost groaned aloud because he had not warned Burman before to keep the suspect facing the inner door. True, Burman could report how the fellow had looked at various points in the examination, but no description would satisfy so much as a single glance at the man. As it was, the three men moved back and forth over Campbell's field of vision. What had happened in the dining room or the lobby before Grosvenor had been brought in could be implied by the first words of the talk.

Grosvenor said: 'Well, gentlemen, this is a pretty to-do. I should like to have an explanation as quickly as possible. I do not wish'—here his voice deepened any grew rich with a human sympathy—'I do not wish to get you in trouble with the management of the hotel but . . .'

'What's your name?' demanded Burman harshly.

'By what authority, in the first place, do you ask me? What is your power to question me?' said Grosvenor.

'Show him the warrant, Steve,' commanded Burman. Then as papers rustled: 'Wait a minute. See if he's gonna refuse to tell us his name. *That's* important, too.'

'I don't refuse my name,' answered Grosvenor. 'But I wish in the first place to understand . . .?'

'He's gonna hold out on us,' said Burman, walking impatiently back and forth across Campbell's field of view. To the bottom of his heart, Campbell was appreciating Burman's bluff. 'We oughta take and drop him in the jail and let him ripen. They ripen 'em fast down there.'

'About ten minutes is all they need to ripen 'em,' said Steve. 'Shall I take him down?'

'If you intend an arrest,' said Grosvenor, 'I demand to know the nature of the charge.'

'Tell him, Steve,' said Burman.

'To hell with him,' answered Steve. 'Why should we treat him better than any low bum, seeing what we know about him?'

Campbell warmed one hand against the

185

other, smiling broadly. He felt a deep sense of gratitude to both of these house detectives.

'All right,' said Burman, 'but I'll try him once more. What's your real name?'

'Albert Gresham,' said Grosvenor. 'And that name . . .'

'. . . can be changed around for Aloysius Grosvenor, eh?' asked Burman.

'Aloysius Grosvenor?' he queried. There was an instant of pause. Burman laughed.

'Aw, why not come clean?' he demanded.

'You speak of coming clean, my friends,' said the magnificent Grosvenor, 'but I wish to tell you that . . .'

'Ah, take it easy,' cautioned Burman. 'Steve, get behind this bozo and keep a gun on him.'

'I protest!' Grosvenor began in a loud voice.

'Go on and protest and be damned,' growled Burman. 'I'm gonna go through you, brother. Keep your hands up as high as your shoulders, will you?'

'This damnable outrage . . .!' shouted Grosvenor.

'Nobody's damned around here,' said Burman, 'except the crooks that wear two pairs of names.'

'That little matter?' said Grosvenor, pouring an oily persuasion into his tones. 'You have to understand that my mother . . .'

'Don't rat it,' advised Burman.

His hands began to move over the stout body of the big man. These hands paused.

'Do I feel something in here?'

'I have a license for it,' declared Grosvenor.

Burman pulled out an old-fashioned, single-action Colt from Grosvenor's clothes.

'What name you got the license under?' he asked shortly.

'What name?' said Grosvenor. 'As a matter of fact, it's under the name of Grosvenor. My proper name, but the other I used to prevent any embarrassment . . .'

'What a big, soggy bum you are, anyway,' said Burman. 'Steve, go telephone New York and ask if there's a gun license there for Aloysius Grosvenor . . .'

'Now that I remember,' said Grosvenor, 'I think that this year I took out the license in Wrayneville.'

'The heck you did!' commented Burman. 'Where's Wrayneville?'

'Wrayneville, Colorado? You must have heard of Wrayneville. No, perhaps you haven't. Wrayneville is a very charming place, delicious air, a great deal of sun . . .'

'You got a gun license there, did you?' asked Burman.

'We Westerners grow in the habit of carrying weapons for self-defense,' said Grosvenor.

'Yeah, and so do a lot of us Middle Westerners,' said Burman, 'and so do a lot of Easterners, too. A pile of them go to the chair every year, they're so damned used to defending themselves . . . How many times you been in jail, Grosvenor?'

'Jail? To whom are you addressing yourself?' squalled Grosvenor.

'I'm asking . . . were you ever in jail, Mister Grosvenor, alias Gresham?'

'My friend,' said Grosvenor, 'I see that you are determined to misunderstand me. A childish prank when I was a boy in school . . . otherwise, certainly I never have been in jail.'

'Why don't you slide him down to jail?' suggested Steve. 'This bozo is somebody that they'd like to talk to. They know how to put on the pressure, and a whole lot of juice could be squeezed out of this sap.'

'We'll just scratch around and see for ourselves,' said Burman.

He continued his search and, in full view of Campbell, pulled out a wallet.

'You can't do that!' shouted Grosvenor.

He made a lunge for Burman who, springing back from the hands of the big fellow, bumped a shoulder against the inner door and flung it wide open. Grosvenor stood staring at the revealed face of Campbell.

'Still smoking those swell cigars?' asked Campbell.

From the corner of his eye he damned the clumsiness of Burman. The house detective, screwing his mouth, made a gesture of despair.

'Ah! . . . I remember you,' said Grosvenor.

'Yeah. You remember me, all right,' answered Campbell. 'How many extra names do you pack with your things, Grosvenor?'

Grosvenor at this moment was magnificent. He held up the flat of his hand and laughed a little, a truly melodious chuckle, as of one honestly amused.

'Ah, that?' he said. 'I want to assure you, Mister Campbell, that the name of Grosvenor is much dearer to me than my person. I would be a pitiable fellow if I permitted that name to be associated with trouble of any sort. These honest fellows have been put on my trail by you, Mister Campbell. But you must have a superior knowledge, as a man of the world, to a . . .'

'Jeez, I'd like to rap him for that,' commented Burman softly.

'Give me the wallet,' said Campbell.

He extended his hand for it, never moving his eyes from the face of Grosvenor. He saw Grosvenor's glance flicker wildly to the side as the wallet came in view again. It was a fat purse, and the stuffing was all in greenbacks. Campbell flicked his thumb over the corner of the stack. All were hundreds and fifties.

'You're sweating, Grosvenor,' he observed. 'What's the matter?'

'Do you think a man will submit to being robbed?' cried Grosvenor. 'Do you imagine a man can stand and see his property handled by strangers who . . .'

'Ah, shut up, mug,' cautioned Burman.

'Why are you sweating?' demanded

189

Campbell again. 'It's running down your face. You look gray and green.'

'For this conduct, you'll be answerable, all three,' said Grosvenor.

'How yellow are you?' asked Campbell. 'There's five thousand dollars here.'

Grosvenor closed his eyes and opened them again.

Steve said: 'Sure, he's no petty larceny bum. He's the goods, he is.'

'Five thousand is a pretty big stack, isn't it?' persisted Campbell.

'As for the money . . .,' said Grosvenor.

'Yes, what about this money?' asked Campbell. 'You didn't have it on the train.'

The whole frame of Grosvenor was shaken by this remark.

'How do you know that?' he cried. 'How do you . . . how did you dare to search . . .?'

'I didn't search,' said Campbell. 'I just know. That's the way with some of us. We just know. Where did you get this five thousand, Grosvenor?'

'I refuse to answer,' said Grosvenor, his face now dripping wet. 'This outrageous inquisition cannot be permitted to . . .'

'Who gave you this money?' Campbell repeated quietly.

'I'll not be bullied into talking,' shouted Grosvenor.

'I don't think you will,' said Campbell. 'But I want to ask you something. Is five thousand enough? Is that a big enough price for murder?'

'Murder?' breathed Grosvenor.

His knees went loose. He got a hand on a chair and sat down with a heavy slump of his body.

'Ay, murder,' said Campbell, stepping close and leaning to study the greasy white face. 'An accessory before the fact . . . you can hang by your fat neck for that, Grosvenor. Understand? Hang by the fat of your throat!'

Grosvenor began to pull himself together. He stood up and towered above them.

'I demand my instant liberation or else instant incarceration and a crime placed against me,' he said. 'As an American citizen, I have that right.'

'Sure he has,' said Steve. 'Leave us take him down to the station and charge him with the gun. Maybe murder'll leak out of him somehow later on.'

Campbell, staring continually into the handsome, strange face, held out the wallet.

'Take it back,' he said. 'I don't want it. Give me the gun, Burman.'

Grosvenor got the wallet in both hands, dragged in a breath, and shoved the money away inside his coat.

'Here's your gat, too,' said Campbell, passing it over.

It disappeared with expert swiftness under the coat of Grosvenor. 'The whole detail of this circumstance is firmly pictured in my mind,' he said, 'and I shall not forget your names, your faces, and every act which has taken place here, and every word that has been spoken.'

'Get out,' said Campbell.

The big fellow pulled a snorting breath, reached the door with a stride, and went out with a sudden jerk of the body, as though he were kicked from behind.

'Why?' growled Burman. 'Why'd you let him go?'

'Tell him, Steve, will you?' asked Campbell. 'Better dodge is to get another one of your boys to look after him. He'd have his eye out for the rest of us. Get somebody on him, will you?' Steve nodded and went out. Campbell sat down, lighted a cigarette, and immediately drew in a long breath of the smoke. He stared down at the floor.

'It beats me,' exploded Burman at last.

'What does?' asked Campbell rather faintly, his thoughts were so far away.

'Why you'd let a skunk like that go.'

'Don't you see?'

'No. I don't see at all. You could sock him in the pen for carrying a gun. They take gun carrying in a big way here in this town.'

'He's a big fellow, isn't he?' asked Campbell.

'Yeah, he's big all right, but is he too big for you?'

'He's big,' said Campbell, 'but the only use

192

he is to me is as a feather.'

'Meaning what?'

'Why, to show which way the wind blows. Steve is a wide-awake fellow, isn't he? He won't let Grosvenor get out of sight, will he?'

'He'll have him tailed. Steve's a bright lad.'

'That's good,' said Campbell, 'because if we don't keep Grosvenor in sight, then I'm done in by this trick . . . I've made a terrible fool of myself.'

'You big time fellows take the big risks, don't you?' said Burman with admiration. 'It beats me the way you go all out. Sometime you'll have a twenty-story fall. The ground'll cut right away from under you.'

Here the door jerked open, and Steve thrust in a startled face.

'I got Jigger Wilson on him, and the Jigger just tells me that he's disappeared. Got into a big sweep of people from the elevators, and Jigger was elbowed back at the front door . . .'

CHAPTER TWENTY-SEVEN

Latimer Treads Softly

There is nothing that makes one so forward-minded as a taxicab in Chicago. The traffic moves with a swerving rush in that town, and the taxicab drivers are inspired devils who seem to think their cars are threads which always can be put through a needle's eye. Passengers regret that their insurance is not larger and wonder why they have never learned to appreciate the pleasures of pedestrianism. All the while they keep their eyes fixed fast forward on the dissolving and reforming currents of the traffic.

Latimer, as he left the station in the cab, sat back with a small hand mirror which he raised just high enough to enable him to study what went on behind the car. He printed on his mind's eye the picture of the machines immediately behind. He studied their radiators until he knew their names, and that was not easy in 1935, where so many drew out to a sharp point, like the bows of a ship. Then he gave the driver a new address and felt the sway as the machine took the next corner to the left.

They went for three blocks, and he studied the traffic again. Half of the cars were sure to be of identical models, of course, but he noticed one long, low, gray affair which was there behind him, two rows back. It had followed before. It still was following.

'Take the shortest cut. Step on it, driver,' called Latimer.

The driver shrugged his shoulders, slid down lower beneath the wheel, and turned the car into a thing with wings. For ten minutes they dodged through the field like a running halfback. Then Latimer studied the traffic behind him again. The long gray car was there again, still two files back. Then they had their speed quenched in the traffic jam of a one-way street. Latimer leaned forward and slipped a bill over the shoulder of the driver.

'I forgot something back there,' he said. 'Leave my bag at the Hotel Chester. Keep the change.'

He stepped out, walked through the jam of cars, and gained the opposite side of the street. Deep in the shadows of the doorway of a closed store, he withdrew and watched the jam break, slowly start. The gray car was among the others. There was no one inside it except a liveried chauffeur. Latimer pursed his forehead and forgot to smile.

He turned the corner, went up three blocks, and took another cab. Again he went with rushes and pauses toward his address. But estimating his progress, he decided that an active man on foot might have kept pace with the taxi, so thick was the press of cars and so long the waits. Still he studied the cars behind him and, as he went on, decided that not one of them was sticking to his trail.

It was not certain, by this time, that he had escaped being tailed, but he decided that the chances were ten to one against. At last he reached the corner he had selected, paid the cab, and went along on foot. Again he turned a corner, stepped back into the twilight of a doorway, and for ten long minutes watched the pedestrians and the automobiles go by him.

When he went on again, it was with few glances behind him, for he was satisfied that he had dodged pursuit. In fact he could not have been expected to study not only his own side of the street but also the opposite sidewalk, where a rather chunky figure walked briskly ahead, waited for the traffic, and went on. When Latimer fell into his proper walking gait, the chunky fellow dropped well back, following at a distance of perhaps half a block. On the few occasions when Latimer turned, the fat man was idling in front of a shop window or talking to one of the children who littered the street as they entered a Negro quarter. Furthermore, the fat man had various attitudes in his walking, and each was different from the others. He was at times affected by a limp, and again he walked briskly, head high, with all the demeanor of one who went whistling on his way, content with the world, or yet again with his collar turned up against the drizzle of the rain he seemed a poor unfortunate without a home or a friend. That, perhaps, was the greatest reason why Latimer, in the doubtful light between day and night, failed to spot that tailer.

The Negro quarter which he had entered was one of those new districts which the black tide had invaded. Before the Great War, Chicago had been districted within certain clear lines and boundaries, but in the post-war

196

years Negro population increased, lured from the South by the reports of high wages. The blacks began to leave their old abodes and press outwards in new directions. Wherever they went, the value of real estate for the whites declined. What was the height of fashion one year was overclouded the next. Cunning landlords bought abandoned property for a song, cut up the big rooms into crowded little apartments, and filled the houses with Negroes. Their individual rents were small, but their numbers were so great that the investments paid hugely.

It was into such a district that Latimer had passed. The evening was cold and wet, but the children were still out at play. In the half light the pavements were filled with faceless men and women who came out of shadows into life only when they were close enough for Latimer to see the flashing whites of their eyes.

He entered a street of dignified houses, leaning shoulder to shoulder, an almost empty block with 'For Sale' signs dimly visible on the front of nearly every one. The whites had removed from that sector only recently, and the blacks had not yet taken their place. It was a sort of No Man's Land—a gloomy air of emptiness and despair in some manner looked out of those tall fronts and depressed the passer-by.

In the middle of the block Latimer turned down the steps to a cellar door and fitted a key

197

into the lock of it. The bolt slid stiffly back. He had to press down before the door gave way a little, yet he managed all with such care that he made no sound. Only the wind entered before him and whistled faintly through the interior.

He took out a pocket torch and slashed the darkness right and left. It had been a servant's room, perhaps. The worthless frame of an old iron cot, together with badly rusted springs, fitted askew into a corner. Near the cot the floor was spotted with black where cigarettes had been allowed to fall and had burned out on the wood. The ceiling was badly cracked and rain-stained at one end. Otherwise there was nothing to note except the dust on the floor, and into that dust Latimer peered closely. It was not thick enough to take a good imprint, but it seemed to him that he made out the dim trail of footprints across the boards.

He slanted the light across them to bring out the definition more clearly. He blew on the delicate edges of the prints and watched the dust dissolve under his breath. Someone, he decided, had entered the house within the last few days. He could come no closer to the time than that, but it was enough to make him go ahead with the greatest caution.

Behind the front bedroom there were four other chambers, each clean swept, the doors ajar. He looked into them, one by one. He entered them and, opening the closet doors, he peered inside with his light and his revolver.

The last room on the cellar floor was a big laundry. He stood only for a moment to scan it with his torch. The light glinted across a huge spiderweb that hung across a window face. Latimer thought how pinched the belly of that lady spider must be in the deserted old house where even the flies would lose interest, after a time, and no longer try to get through the crevices into the interior, lured by the smell of food.

There was no odor now except a damp mustiness together with a faint stain in the air that lingers so long after human habitation—as though the walls and the floor had soaked it up and then gave it out again by degrees, for years and years. The cellar steps were finished and painted wood. He went up them, treading close to the wall where the heavy weight of his body would act on a shorter leverage and would not be apt to make the boards creak. At the head of the straight flight was another door, also locked. The same key which had opened the outer cellar door fitted in this one also. It was not swollen with damp but gave inwards at the first touch of his hand.

He was now in the hallway on the first floor. Every door, right and left, was closed. So he started at the left. The doors were closed but not locked. The first one he opened held the empty shelves of what had once been a library, with a deep, bricked fireplace. Next came a long living room that ran on to the front of the dwelling. When he turned his torch ray up, it was multiplied into a million brilliant particles, for a big chandelier had been left hanging from the center of the ceiling. The new fashion was against chandeliers, and he wondered why it had been left. Because it had value, it seemed to Latimer, like a living thing, abandoned here by a cruel folly.

This side of the first floor was empty. He passed across the hall. Here the door stuck a little. He had to lift up hard before it came clear and, opening wide upon the room, let in a damp breath of draught about his head and shoulders. More than this attracted him. In the air of the room there was the stale, disagreeable odor of cigarette smoke.

People had been in that room not long before, within a few hours in fact. A little deal table occupied the center of the floor. There was a stool on one side of it, and two broken chairs were nearby. Three people, perhaps, had been conferring here. Thrusting his head around the corner of the door, he cut the darkness of the ends of the room with the ray of the torch. All, so far as he could see, was empty, but there was a closet at one end to be examined, and there were two deep window embrasures at the front end of the dining room.

He walked gingerly towards the table, picking up and putting down his feet with separate acts of the mind, until a sidecut with his torch glinted on a bright bit of metal in the second embrasure. The light winked out in the hand of Latimer. He took one swift, silent step to the side, dropped to a knee.

The silence continued for a long moment. He might, perhaps, have withdrawn from the room, feeling his way to the hall door. Instead, he began to move very stealthily towards the second embrasure. He rounded the table, reached the further wall, and moved on little by little. His outstretched hand touched the cold marble front of a fireplace. It regained the rough plaster of the wall's face. Still he stalked forward.

'Where are you, Charlie?' called a sudden voice.

'Ah, Pete Winslow!' exclaimed Latimer, and snapped a flood of light into the face of Pete himself, still standing in the embrasure, still with the gun in his hand.

CHAPTER TWENTY-EIGHT

Gathering of a Clan

Pete Winslow, leaning a hand against the wall, nodded and grinned at the big fellow.

'I kind of thought that you'd back out of the place,' he said. 'I kind of thought that you'd slide back into the hall. But when a cat smells a canary, it just follows its nose. I should've guessed that.'

He began to laugh. He licked his lips and stared earnestly at Latimer. 'Like father, like son,' he commented.

'Why didn't you speak up when you saw that it was I?' asked Latimer.

'I dunno,' said Pete. 'I was just wondering if you *were* like your old man, that never took a backward step. I remember down in the Patridge Saloon when there was big Joe McCarthy and Sid Devon, and three more that come in looking for your old man.'

'I've heard that story,' Latimer interrupted. 'Where's Champion?'

'Here, your honor,' said the husky voice of Champion.

Latimer turned quickly about on him. 'What's the matter with you fellows?' he asked. 'Are you trying to make a fool of me?'

'How could we make a fool of a man that's spent so much time in school?' asked Champion. He took off his hat and rubbed the flat of his hand over his bald head and grinned.

'What have you swallowed, the pair of you?' asked Latimer. 'What makes you act so fat and foolish anyway?'

'Why,' said Pete, in his genial way, 'it's just realizin' that we got a Latimer with us. That's what makes us happy. It would make *anybody* happy, wouldn't it?'

'Sit down,' commanded Latimer.

'Take a chair, Champ,' ordered Pete. 'I wanta walk around and stretch a little. I was kind of nervous staying there in the dark, waiting for the big cat to creep up on me ... Look it here, Charlie. What would you have done if you'd found me in the dark? Not knowing who it was, what would you have done?'

With the cold, faint smile, Latimer continued to regard him. At last he said: 'Sit down, Pete.'

Pete obeyed.

Champion pulled a flask out of his pocket. 'Have a shot, Charlie?' he asked.

'Where did you get that stuff?' demanded Latimer.

'Just picked it up off the street,' said Champion.

'Where did you get it?' asked Latimer, raising his voice not in pitch but in volume.

'Why, just outside of town. There was a little joint along the way. Me and Pete felt kind of cold.'

'You'll feel a damned sight colder when you've been hanging up by the neck for a couple of hours,' said Latimer.

'Charlie, you're enough to give a gent bad dreams,' observed Champion.

'You've raised hell, the pair of you,' said Latimer. 'And you're old and in your dotage. You sit here laughing like a pair of old fools.'

'You can't help that,' answered Pete. 'When

a fellow gets old, his brains gets old with him, right?'

'Yes, the brains get old,' said Champion.

Both he and Pete were so highly delighted that they hardly could contain themselves. And big Latimer, with his faint smile, looked back and forth from one face to another.

'They've had plenty of chances to see you,' said Latimer at last. 'That's one reason you're so happy. That's the real reason. What you'd like best of all would be to have your pictures in the papers. You'd like that, wouldn't you, Pete?'

'Some folks have told me that I got kind of an interesting face at that,' said Pete.

'You've been using an interesting gun, too,' said Latimer. 'As though there wasn't enough hell around us, you've had to use a gun!'

'I didn't shoot to kill,' said Pete complacently. 'I seen the big gent and just drilled him through the leg, high up. It kind of discourages most folks when they get drilled through the leg, like that. But the kid was Irish. He tried to come right in on us, and then he fell and whanged his head. It wasn't the shooting that might've killed him, but him being such a nervy young damned fool.'

'When you get to hellfire's edge,' said Latimer, 'you'll still have excuses . . . you'll still have reasons why you shouldn't burn.'

'A man has to talk,' said Pete. 'You know that, Charlie. We ain't all like you and your father before you, that can keep our mouths shut so good.'

'Were you followed after you brought the airplane down?' asked Latimer.

'Not a bit that we could see. We headed back south and showed ourselves a coupla places so's the other boys would be fooled.'

'That was good enough,' said Latimer, 'if they don't find out where you doubled.'

'Even O'Rourke ain't likely to find us,' remarked Champion.

'Who's that? Oh, Campbell's partner on the train . . .'

'Who's Campbell?' asked Pete.

'The hardest Scotchman you ever saw, and the smartest,' admitted Latimer. 'He's made of tool-proof steel with a diamond finish . . . I'd expect anything of him.'

'He may be a fine head,' said Pete, 'but O'Rourke is a funny kind of devil. He thinks out your thoughts for you. After I seen him a couple times, I was scared to do any thinking for fear that he'd read what was in my head. You'd think he was too fat to have a head on him, but he's quick with the old brain. I'm glad we've shaken him off, Champ.'

'If we'd busted his head wide open, it wouldn't've been bad,' observed Champion.

'When you bought that whiskey, were you traveling south?' asked Latimer.

'No, we were comin' on towards Chicago,' said Pete.

'Then they'll pick up your trail at that point,' observed Latimer. 'You had to have the whiskey, did you?'

'It was kind of a time to celebrate, wasn't it, Charlie?' asked Champion with some anxiety.

'That kind of celebrating will put you in jail,' said Latimer.

'Pete kind of misses jail anyway,' said Champion, and he laughed again.

Into this laughter Pete fell. Regarding one another, the two veterans tilted back their heads and indulged themselves until the tears went down their faces. And Latimer, high of head, patient, examined their faces.

He said at last: 'You have it?'

'Have what?' asked Champion, wiping his eyes.

'You have the plan,' said Latimer.

'How would we get that?' demanded Pete innocently.

'You'd get it out of the rathouse where Cobb was living,' said Latimer, eyeing them still.

'Well,' said Pete, 'we looked all through his things, but we couldn't find it.'

'You couldn't?' said Latimer.

'We couldn't find it,' said Champion, shaking his head.

Latimer lighted a cigarette and blew the smoke straight ahead of him. He reached up a swift, impatient hand and cut the draught of smoke in two.

Afterwards, he stared into the bright,

mocking eyes of the two elders.

'You found the plan,' he insisted quietly. 'I can tell by the look of you.'

'We didn't find it,' declared Pete. 'O'Rourke found it for us.'

'O'Rourke?'

'Ay, it was O'Rourke that found it for us. One day, we might send a present to him. He's a brainy man and only a little crooked.'

'How crooked?' asked Latimer.

'He wanted to come in with us.'

'I guess he was only stringing us,' commented Pete a moment later, as he thought the matter out. 'He just wanted to start us talking. A fellow like O'Rourke wouldn't touch crooked money unless he got it through political graft or something like that. Just good enough to be bad is the way with his kind.'

'Give me the plan,' put in Latimer.

The two looked at one another. 'He says he wants it,' interrupted Pete.

Champion nodded his head. 'He thinks he ought to have it,' he agreed.

'Why should you have it, Charlie?' asked Pete.

'Because the pair of you will be in jail, inside of another couple of days,' explained Latimer.

'The boys would trust you to keep out of trouble?'

The smile of Latimer went out, and that hard, still look of disgust entered his eyes.

'I always stay out of trouble,' he said.

'Yeah, and he does,' said Pete, sighing. 'He wouldn't've been back in the hands of O'Rourke three times, like we were. Or me, anyway.'

'O'Rourke had glue on his hands. You couldn't get away from him,' answered Champion.

'Give me the plan,' said Latimer.

Pete shrugged his shoulders, whistled a dreary note, and then reached inside his coat. Latimer reached his own hand inside his coat and waited, tense.

'You think I'm grabbing for a gun?' asked Pete curiously.

'You might be,' said Latimer.

'You wouldn't trust me, eh?'

'No more than I'd trust poison snakes.'

'Listen, boys,' said Champion. 'You wouldn't be arguin', would you?'

'Be still, Champ,' commanded Latimer, keeping his cold eyes on Pete.

'Why should I trust you, then?' asked Pete.

'Because you know that the thing would be safer with me. That's the only reason.'

'He's right,' said Champion.

'Yeah,' drawled Pete. 'I suppose that's true. I suppose that he's right.'

He pulled out the fold of paper and pushed it gingerly across the table. Latimer opened it and glanced it over.

'Did O'Rourke see this?' he asked.

'Yes. He saw it, all right. He found it,' said Champion.

'Damn,' muttered Latimer.

He lighted a match, held up the paper, and applied the flame to a corner of it.

Pete yelled out as though he had been struck with a knife. Champion lurched from his chair, grabbing. But Latimer caught them by the wrists and held them easily.

He said: 'Let it burn. We don't need it now.'

The paper wafted to the floor. They could hear the tiny crinkling noise of the flames, so perfect was the silence of the moment.

'Why don't we need it, for cat's sake?' demanded Pete.

'Because I've got it drawn down in my memory now,' said Latimer.

'The figures and the angles and everything?' cried Champion.

'The figures and the angles and everything,' said big Latimer.

A gust of wind struck the house. Latimer turned his head and listened.

'Yeah, maybe you can remember them,' nodded Pete. 'That's better than having the stuff on paper that can be grabbed.'

Latimer, lifting his hand for silence, stole with soundless, flowing steps to the door, caught hold of it, and tore it suddenly open. Josephine Worth pitched inward into his arms.

CHAPTER TWENTY-NINE

Oil and Water

Big Charles Latimer gave the girl only a glance
and then passed her into the room. Afterwards
he made a cautious step onto the threshold of
the doorway and glanced his torch up and
down the hall.

He turned, closed the door behind him, and
heard Pete Winslow saying: 'Hello, Jo. Now,
dog-gone me but I'm glad to see you. Who you
got along with you?'

'Hello, Jo,' said the unctuous voice of
Champion. 'This is mighty fine. Never seen so
much color in your face before.'

She was smiling at them and shaking hands.

'Who brought you here?' asked Pete.

'I came by myself,' said the girl.

'Now look here, honey,' said Pete, 'I allow
you're a mighty brave girl, but you wouldn't be
hunting ground by yourself all through black
town, would you?'

'I didn't have to hunt,' said the girl. 'I knew
that his father owned this house. I could guess
where you'd show up.'

'That sounds more reasonable,' said
Champion. 'Still, you must've taken somebody
along, Jo. You wouldn't go prying all alone into

an empty house, would you?'

'She'd be able to come alone,' announced Latimer. 'She'd be able to do anything, alone. Look at her now. D'you think that she's afraid of the dark?'

The girl had turned to Latimer with her head thrown high, her face cold as stone.

'You sure look kind of resolved, Jo,' remarked Champion.

She altered at once. She threw out both hands to Latimer and cried out: 'Charles, why do you treat me as though I were a poisonous beast?'

Latimer's faint smile did not alter. He looked her up and down with a quiet detestation.

'No,' he said, 'not a beast. The beasts don't have the sort of brains you carry around with you. Sit down.'

She obeyed that command, slipping into a chair with her head down, inert as though she had been struck from her feet by his words.

'Hold on, Charlie. Don't be so damned mean,' said Pete. 'A gal as pretty as Jo . . . you don't act hardly human to her.'

'Lift your head,' directed Latimer.

She dropped it still lower.

He put his big, brown hand under her chin and raised her head. Tears made her eyelashes glisten. Her lips seemed to tremble.

'Look at her,' said Latimer. 'It's wonderful, isn't it? I've seen the great ones of the stage

211

work themselves into real tears. But she doesn't have to work. She presses a button, and the tears are there.'

She struck his hand away with both of hers.

'I despise you,' she said, half whispering the words.

'That's more like it,' said Latimer. 'Did you see her face, just now? See how the baby went out of her eyes, and the devil came into them? How would you like to meet a face like that on a dark night?'

She drew a handkerchief from her sleeve and dabbed her eyes with it. Leaning back in the chair with her lips slightly parted, she breathed like one exhausted.

'There's the fourth change,' remarked Latimer. 'Now, I ask you, why should a talent like that be wasted? Why the devil shouldn't she be on the stage where the millions could see her and adore her? Why does she have to be simply a crook?'

'Charles,' murmured the girl. 'Please.'

'She'll have tears again in a moment,' said Latimer. 'You can trust her for that. There . . . see 'em come?'

'Pete, will you make him stop?' asked the girl, making a suddenly pleading gesture towards Winslow.

'Ain't you kind of ashamed of yourself, Charlie?' asked Pete, with a great deal of curiosity in his manner of asking.

'She's a sweet thing, isn't she, Pete?'

212

demanded Latimer. 'She's nothing but sweet, would you say?'

'I dunno know much about gals,' said Pete.

'Neither do I,' said Latimer. 'Thank my stars, neither do I. This one is enough for me. Just thinking about her will keep me away from the females as long as I live . . . Jo, listen to me.'

She turned her head. She looked up at him with wide, wet eyes.

'Yes, Charles?' she said.

His mouth twitched. He compressed his lips. 'How can you be the way you are?' he demanded.

'What way, Charles?' she asked with a helpless gesture.

'Bah,' he sneered at her. 'Every time you look in the mirror, don't you see what you could have made yourself? Stop playing that damned part. Be yourself and get your head up. Do you think you win anything from me, when you act this way? Why don't you wash your hands as clean as you can get them and try to make a new start?'

'Will you help me to, Charles?' she asked.

He stepped back with an animal grunt of disgust.

'There you are,' he said to Pete. 'No matter what you do, she's always on the stage. And she can play the real parts, too. Up to murder. Up to murder!'

Pete and Champion watched the girl with

steady, bright eyes and said nothing.

'Get out of here,' commanded Latimer. 'I'm sick at the sight of you. Get up and get out of the house.'

'Wait a minute, old-timer,' said Champ. 'Ain't she got a kind of right to talk with us?'

'Didn't she have her old man in the business?' suggested Pete.

'Her father was a decent man,' said Latimer. 'But there's none of his blood in her. Let her be cut in for her share. But keep her out of my way.'

'He's kind of got his back up,' said Pete. 'Maybe you better go, like he says, Jo.'

She jumped out of her chair and cried out furiously at them: 'You are going to let him be the head of everything? What right has he to give the orders? You're both older. You're worth twice a Charles Latimer.'

'Now I like her best,' said Latimer with the half-closed eyes of a connoisseur. 'When she picks up the fire and throws it in one's face. That's when she's at her best.'

She turned on him to add: 'A great, lounging, self-assured hulk ... a chunk of cannon meat ... and you treat him as though he were something to look up to.'

'Well,' said Pete, 'I'm kind of short, and it's easy for me to look up to people. I don't have to sag at the knees none. It just comes natural.'

'Leave the house,' said Latimer. 'If you don't get out of your own volition, I'll carry you

214

out.'

'I don't think you'll do that,' said the girl. She was white faced, her nostrils trembling with her excitement.

'Are you going to march through that door?' demanded Latimer bitterly.

'Not a step,' she answered.

He strode to her and, standing behind her, took her by the elbows.

'Pete ... Champ!' she gasped over her shoulder.

'He looks kind of big and young. I'd do what he says, if I was you,' answered Champ.

'You better go along with him, honey,' said Pete.

'I'll go,' she answered. 'Will you take your hands away?'

'I'm glad if I never have to touch you,' said Latimer, but he followed her to the door.

'I'll go alone,' she said.

'I'll see that you get outside the place,' answered Latimer.

She turned there in the doorway and looked back and up to him, her face stone white and her eyes blazing. Then she went on through the outer hall, carving her path through the darkness with the penciled ray from a very small flashlight.

She went down the steps into the cellar. The shadowy bulk of Latimer followed behind her with that soft, padding step which was peculiar to him. When they reached the door, she turned suddenly into his arms.

'Charles, will you please listen to me for five minutes?' she pleaded. 'I'll tell you every step of my life.'

'I've read Dante,' said Latimer. 'I don't care a great deal about the dirt in your own personal hell . . .' He pushed open the door. 'Get out!'

Josephine whirled quickly away from him and hurried down the street. She walked briskly around the corner, up the block to the left, and turned again onto the street behind that where Latimer's house stood.

She went on to the mid-block narrow alley—a relic of very old building days—and hurried down it. It stopped at a high board fence. She rolled skirt and slip to her hips and went over the fence like a boy. Only at the top of the fence she delayed long enough to scan the rear views of the houses before her. Latimer's place she picked, numbering the houses from the corner to the right spot. Then she dropped down into the back yard. There were two other fences to climb before she would reach her goal.

But she set about her work with a perfectly cool confidence. It was only when she had reached the rear of the house that she paused again to right her clothes and pull the skirt down snugly about her hips. After that she went forward again with her graceful dancer's step.

CHAPTER THIRTY

Invasion

When Campbell found that Aloysius Grosvenor hat escaped from him, he endured the pain of that disappointment for a long moment. Then, rousing himself, he rose from his chair.

Burman said: 'Maybe that feather blew farther off than you expected?'

'I'm just a poor, old damned fool,' said Campbell quietly and walked from the office.

He went to the mail desk first and found at last a small envelope addressed to him, unsealed, and with the telephone message written down: MR. PATRICK TELEPHONED TO ASK YOU TO MEET HIM AT THE CORNER OF BEAUREGARD AND NARCISSUS STREETS.

He smiled faintly at the slight alias under which O'Rourke had chosen to disguise himself. He tossed the note into a waste paper basket, thought better of that, reclaimed it, and tore it to shreds. Then he went out to the entrance of the hotel.

He said to a doorman: 'Have you seen a man go out . . . big, swaggering, eyebrows held away up high? Looks as though something was surprising him?'

'Not seen him, sir,' the doorman returned.

'Seen a thin, small fellow with a white bit of tape across his upper lip?' asked Campbell.

'Not seen him. Sorry, sir,' said the doorman.

'Where's Beauregard and Narcissus?'

'That's a colored residence section now, sir.'

Campbell got a cab and started. The night was growing much colder. The speed of the car sent the air whistling through cracks about the windows, and yet the air within remained stale, and the draughts seemed like cold, dead fingers laid upon his flesh.

He would take up buttermilk and whole wheat bread. He would have oatmeal for cereal every morning. He would heap the cereal with cream and gradually put some fat upon this wasted body of his. At the thought of cream his belly crawled in him. But a man must have more flesh when he grows old. It robes one with greater dignity. That was why O'Rourke, no doubt, captured the greater number of headlines in the newspapers. He had the front of an important fellow.

Halfway to the place of the appointment Campbell remembered an important thing left undone. He stopped at the first saloon and from the telephone booth rang New York. The police call went swiftly through. Corrigan's familiar, snarling voice came over the wire.

'What's the word about the killing?' asked Campbell.

'I'm expecting that from you,' snapped

218

Corrigan. 'Where are those two devils? Where are you?'

'Chicago. I'm on a different trail. The killer I'm talking about is back there in Nineteen Oh Three. Peter Winslow. Who did Peter Winslow kill?'

'I've got it here,' replied Corrigan. After a moment, he said: 'It was a man named Jay Markham ... I've got the whole case written up here. Want any of it?'

'All the main points.'

'It wasn't a saloon fight. That's why the sentence was so long. They didn't think much of a gunfight out there in Willoughby, it looks like. Not so long as it was flavored with whiskey. But this one was out in the open. There were seven partners ...'

'Worth, Latimer, Winslow, and the rest?'

'That's right. Markham was one of them. Jay Markham. All those seven people threw in together. Markham and Winslow went out prospecting together. Only Winslow came back. A rumor went around that he'd found a wonderfully rich vein. It was a whisper that went through the town. No assay report was published, of course. But the story started going. When Markham was found dead, people thought that Winslow had killed him so as to keep the strike secret and work it for himself, later on. That was why Winslow got sent to the pen for life.'

'How did Winslow get out?'

'Pardoned,' said Corrigan.

'Governor pardoned him?'

'Yes.'

'For what? New evidence about the old shooting scrape?'

'That governor maybe could have been bought off,' said Corrigan. 'The story in the inside circle out there is that John Cobb was able to get to the governor and bought off Winslow.'

'Cobb bought him off?' shouted Campbell, his brain ringing with excitement.

'That makes a good circle, don't it?' said Corrigan.

'Good? It's beautiful!' cried Campbell. 'Anything else?'

'Nothing very important. I'll read the whole report to you, if you want.'

'That's enough,' said Campbell. 'I can go on that, I guess. There's no mention of a Grosvenor in the yarn anywhere?'

'No.'

'Nor of a Gresham?'

'Not a word.'

'It's damned funny . . . but let it go. I'll carry on. Corrigan, we're not quite in the dark. We've got a little light to go by.'

'Good, Angus,' said the inspector. 'The papers are carrying this big. They're making it big time stuff. Fifteen millions . . . burned alive in an iron chair . . . airplanes forced down and all that . . . the whole town is full of it. Angus, if

220

you two make anything of this, you'll get into department history.'

When Campbell had rung off and returned to his cab, he was sitting erect on the edge of his seat, shuddering with excitement. The tremor remained in him when the cab stopped on the corner of Beauregard and Narcissus. He paid it off and watched the red tail light bob out of view around the next corner. He lingered for a moment near a street light, letting his loitering be explained by a very deliberate igniting of a cigarette.

It seemed to Campbell, as he waited there, that a shadow slipped out of view near a house front farther up the street, but he was by no means sure of this. The match flame had cast such a dazzle into his eyes.

'This way, Angus,' O'Rourke's voice called from the black darkness.

He stepped back into the shadow beside a low porch. He could spot the familiar fumes of an O'Rourke cigar before he could make out the man. A moment later he was peering under the steps, through the arch in front of the cellar door. There was the glow of the cigar butt.

'News?' said Campbell.

'Yes, news. Gimme yours.'

'Grosvenor got five thousand dollars from Lawrence Purvis Pelton.'

'He did? Then it's Grosvenor and Pete and Champion!' exclaimed O'Rourke.

'*And* a gold mine, *and* Cobb's millions, and

Pelton paying for the murder. It's big, Pat.'

'Don't let it go to your head,' said O'Rourke.

'To *my* head?' answered Campbell angrily.

'I was scared of it from the first,' said O'Rourke. 'Fifteen millions is a lot for one Scotch head to keep thinking about. But let that go . . .'

'I'm damned if I let it go,' said Campbell. 'If an Irish bog jumper . . .'

'Will you shut up and listen? I tailed Latimer. He ducked and twisted and doubled like a fox, but I followed him. By car and then on foot. I ran till I was blind, but I spotted the house he went into.'

'Where?'

'Up there across the street. I've been watching it ever since except for stepping into a saloon around the corner and telephoning to the Clifton. Number Twenty-One Eighteen. That's where Latimer went.'

'What's in the house?'

'It's empty, far as I can make out. There's a for sale sign on it. Empty of furniture, I mean. I took a squint through one of the cellar windows and slid a ray of light inside. Empty of furniture, but not of people. Latimer's still in there. Miss Josephine Worth isn't.'

'Has she been around?'

'I saw her come out and go down the street. I spotted her when she went under that street light yonder . . . Where's Grosvenor?'

'I let him have the money back,' explained Campbell. 'He's as guilty as hell, but he's not

222

the only one. I figured that if I turned him loose, he'd lead me to something big. Besides, what have we got on him except money from Pelton? Pelton was hiding behind the name of Purvis. He and Grosvenor are not friends. They hate each other...! I thought I might scoop in Grosvenor and Purvis and the whole gang if we held back a little. They'll certainly get in touch with Pete and Champion. But the fool of a detective in the hotel let Grosvenor get away. He slipped.'

'What about the Scotch fool that left the shadowing to a hotel dick?' exclaimed O'Rourke.

'How was I to know that the jackass couldn't do his work? There was a crowd ...!'

'I don't give a hang about the explanations. Grosvenor's gone, is he?'

'And he's guilty as hell. He sweated green when I told him that we can send accessories before the fact of murder to the chair.'

'It's Grosvenor, is it?' muttered O'Rourke. 'I hoped that we could get something bigger than that fathead on the hook.'

'We will,' agreed Campbell. 'You have Latimer spotted. The whole gang will show up together ... perhaps in that same house. Is there a back entrance?'

'I don't know. I suppose so. Anyway, the girl used the front cellar door. Why wouldn't Latimer use it then?'

'Because he's different from other people,' said Campbell. 'I've seen some of the things he's done, and he's different. There's news from Nevada. I just got it. Winslow went up for life for shooting one of his six partners. Jay Markham. Something about a rich mining strike. John Cobb bought Winslow out of jail. Bribery of the governor or something like that, the people on the inside say. Do you begin to get the picture?'

'I get it. I get it,' said O'Rourke. He puffed his cigar so excitedly that the smacking of his lips was audible. Campbell shuddered with disgust.

'Can't you smoke except you make a sound like a pig eating apples?' he asked.

'Shut up and be still,' said O'Rourke. 'I'm thinking about that back way into the house. It's gotta be covered.'

'It ought to be,' said Campbell.

'If Latimer's in there, we ought to be in there, too,' said O'Rourke.

'We should,' agreed Campbell. 'I wish there was more of us.'

'I never seen you show fear of any man, Angus. What's the matter with you?' asked O'Rourke.

'Latimer. He's different. He'd strangle the two of us like that, Pat.'

'Maybe. Maybe,' said O'Rourke, who had an Irishman's dislike of being considered inferior to anyone in the world.

'It'll be splitting up, if one of us goes around behind,' said Campbell.

'We've got to do it,' said O'Rourke. 'Wait five minutes for me. I'm going around behind the block and try to come in through the back

224

yards. You try to get in from the front. Will you do that, Angus?'

'Ay, will I?' said Campbell. 'If that devil Latimer comes in sight of you, don't stop to question. Shoot, Pat!'

'I will,' said O'Rourke and left instantly to perform his part of the task.

Campbell, however, waited for a moment as had been agreed. Besides, he wanted to rouse himself, for he was one of those cold-blooded men who increase their fervor by gradual degrees and have a high flashpoint.

He crossed the street, therefore, after some four or five minutes had elapsed. The door was locked, but a window gave readily to his hand, and he wriggled over into the darkness. That window made a clumsy point of retreat, however, so he found the door again and turned the key. He even pulled the door a little ajar before he turned again and started down the hall.

There were only windy whispers in that big house. The occasional rays from his pocket light as he switched it on and off startled him when they fell on the emptiness ahead. It was not a sound that he heard then but a mere shadow over his mind like the flick of a bat's wing. He stiffened, turning his torch on to full blaze, and he looked over his shoulder in time to see, dimly, the contorted face of Aloysius Grosvenor rushing upon him.

CHAPTER THIRTY-ONE

Murder in the House

The height and weight of Grosvenor overwhelmed Campbell at the first impact and hurled him on his face with his arms spread out flat on the floor. The bulk about him crushed the wind from his narrow lungs. The flashlight, clattering against the floor, went out. Then there was the thick, dark silence, with Grosvenor breathing hard and making a queer, moaning sound of content.

The big, gasping whisper said: 'By God, Campbell, there's going to be one less bright detective in the world. You hear me?'

'I hear,' said Campbell.

For it was best to talk, he knew. Silence will make the devil in a man leap on tiptoe.

'How is it now, Campbell? Who's sweating now?'

'I'm the one that sweats now, Grosvenor,' he admitted.

Grosvenor drew in such a breath that it whistled through his teeth with a sound as though he were sucking up water.

'I've got the gun ready, Campbell,' he said. 'You hear it tap on the floor?'

'I hear it,' agreed Campbell.

'You're going to die, Campbell. And I'm going to watch your face.'

He took out a torch, snapped on the switch, and laid it on the floor. The light flared into Campbell's eyes.

'What a wizened mug you've got,' said Grosvenor. 'How much hell have you pried your way into anyway? How many poor devils have you done in? You've done the last of 'em, Campbell. I've got your head on the anvil, and here it goes smash. I pull up your coat over your head, so that the blood and brains won't splatter me, and nothing touches the butt of the gun. I arrange it like this, with the flap back so that I can still see your face. Are you afraid, you Scotch blood-sucker?'

'There's no fear of you in me!' Campbell cried. 'A man can't fear a rat, no matter how big it's bloated.'

'Ah?' said Grosvenor. 'Then take this, damn you!'

*　　　*　　　*

O'Rourke, working his way from the back of the block, followed very much the same course that Josephine Worth had discovered, except that his fat body did not permit him to climb the fences with her athletic ease. As he rolled over the top of them on his thick stomach, he gasped and cursed his luck.

The back yards, fortunately, were empty, so

227

that he had little to stumble over, for the only light that reached him was the small broken rays from the rear of the houses on the farther street. He came behind his goal and tried the cellar windows, one by one. They were all fast. He was panting and so impatient that he swore never again to go on strange missions without carrying with him that comfort of burglars—a diamond point with which to cut the glass of window panes. Backing up, he scanned the rear of the house more thoroughly. There was a drainpipe from the eaves which ran down the wall, and a lighter body and a stronger grip than his own might have climbed it. However, even if he were to climb above, perhaps all the windows would be found securely locked.

Reluctantly he gave up the rear as a means of ingress, though he was forced to admit that it remained perfectly simple for an active man to open any of those windows and descend. In his youth, he told himself, he would not have submitted so easily. But now, with a mournful shake of the head, he turned to the right and followed the narrow concrete path which girdled the house and separated it from the sheer wall of its neighbor.

From the inside he heard nothing, but Campbell must be in there by this time. He thought of Angus Campbell burrowing like a mole through the thick darkness, and the picture in his mind of that withered, stealthy, active body was very pleasant to O'Rourke. He turned the corner of the building into the sunken walk, beneath the street level, that passed the front cellar door. That was when a whisper of sound, a slight grating of running feet came past him, straight out the door. O'Rourke reached with one hand for the shoulder of the small man who broke out from the cellar. With the other hand he drew his gun.

Such was the impetus of that contact that he was dragged, half stumbling, out onto the pavement. There his struggling victim fell, face up, and he looked down at the narrow, dark features of a small man who had a white streak of tape across the upper lip.

The headlight of a passing car at the same moment flashed from the dimmers to full power. It swerved to the curb with a soft, silent rush.

'Up,' said O'Rourke. 'Who are you, and where are you from?'

The slender fellow scrambled to his feet, with O'Rourke's hand assisting him by gripping hard to the scruff of the neck.

He put his hands to his face and groaned: 'In there. He's dead. He's dead. It's murder.'

Out of that car at the curb a stream of four burly policemen advanced on rubber-padded heels towards O'Rourke. They spilled out suddenly around the pair.

'What sort of dirt are you tryin' to kick up here?' asked one of them.

'I'm First Grade Detective O'Rourke,' he

answered, 'from New York.'

'I'm Alexander the Great from Omaha,' said one of the cops, laughing. 'What sort of cheese are you tryin' to feed us, brother?'

'You cross-eyed jackass,' roared O'Rourke, 'if you don't believe your ears, will you believe your eyes? Here's a man that's talking murder. Hold him, a couple of you. Let me see . . .'

He started down the steps from the street level. Two of the police collared him at once.

'Oh, that's an old gag, friend,' said one of them. 'You'll come along with us, First Grade Detective O'Rourke from Omaha!'

'Here,' said O'Rourke patiently, though he was going mad. 'There's a light showing inside. Will you go straight on and arrest every man that you find in the house? Arrest me too, for the fools you are, if you think you have to.'

'He means something,' said one of them. 'Let's go on with him, Jack.'

They went with O'Rourke through the gaping door of the cellar and saw before them as ugly a sight as ever a man witnessed. Jack had snapped on a powerful flashlight as they came to the dinginess of the cellar, and it was into the cone of this that Campbell walked, with his blind hands extended before him, and his face streaming blood.

O'Rourke was freed of the two hands that held him in an instant. He ran to Campbell and caught him by the shoulders.

'Angus, man,' he said. 'Have they murdered

230

you, lad? Have they done you in? Oh, the devils. I'll have 'em burned by inches!'

'Gimme a handkerchief to wipe my eyes,' snapped Campbell angrily. 'Who talks about me being murdered? I'm only choked and blinded in the blood of a swine. There he lies back there . . . Grosvenor. He's burning in hell already, because it would take him only one step from death to get right there.'

He mopped the red from his face quite calmly and led the way back into the narrows of the hall.

There lay Grosvenor, face down, with the hilt of a knife sticking out of his back, and a handkerchief wrapped around it. The turn of his head showed his face with the lips still furled back from his teeth as though he were trying to sink his teeth into the floor. In contrast with that fury was the glazed content of the half-opened eyes.

One of the police, dropping to a knee, slipped a hand under the body to feel the heart.

'He's done,' he said. 'A kind of a damned pretty murder this one makes, too. What I mean, the crook leaves his handkerchief to help us find him. That's kind of nice of him, Sergeant, eh?'

'Nice be damned,' said the sergeant. 'I'd rather have the fingerprints than all the handkerchiefs in the world. Who's this man? Who knows about it?'

'Will you pipe down?' said O'Rourke, 'or do you wanta raise the house?'

'The house is empty,' said the sergeant, looking about him.

'The house ain't empty,' O'Rourke contradicted.

'What's in it, then?' demanded the sergeant.

'Murder down here . . . and murder upstairs, I guess,' said O'Rourke.

He pushed his identifying badge under the nose of the sergeant. 'What happened, Angus?' he demanded solicitously.

'I come here . . . I feel a wind come up behind me . . . it's Grosvenor that whams me down on the floor, lies all over me, and turns on his light that's still shining in his face, so's he could see the look on my face when he mashed my brains out. I think he's ready to hit, and then the weight of him spills out loose and warm as blubber all over me. I don't try to do a thing for a minute. Then I start wriggling. I get out from under and see him the way you see him. It was the spilling of the damned pig's blood in my face that started me squirming.'

'You saw nothing?' asked the sergeant. 'When that man collapsed on top of you . . .?'

'Will you keep your voice down, Sergeant dear?' asked O'Rourke, 'or do you want every murdering devil in the house to know that the law is on their heels?'

He grinned with fury at the sergeant, who scowled and tucked his face down deeper

232

between his walrus jowls.

'How could I see anything?' said Campbell, 'I was lyin' on the floor, face down, waiting for murder. All I know is that the man spilled out all loose over me, and then I thought I heard feet whispering along the floor, light as a girl running, and then a door closed somewhere, I thought.'

The sergeant was only half listening to this talk, for he was picking up the handkerchief that was wrapped around the handle of the knife.

'A. G.' said the sergeant. 'It's got A. G. stitched into the corner. Find an A. G. and you've got the man that did this killing.'

'His name is Aloysius Grosvenor, the man that's lying there,' said O'Rourke, 'and that proves that he reached around and stabbed himself in the back. But he didn't want to leave the fingermarks. Maybe he didn't want any of the dirty blood on his hands. So he wrapped the knife up before he stabbed. How's that for a theory, Angus?'

'It's a damned good theory,' said Campbell. 'I never heard a better one. But bless the person that slid that knife into the back of murdering Aloysius Grosvenor. D'you see the arch of his eyebrows, Angus? He's still surprised at what he's seeing in hell.'

'Everybody pipe down,' said O'Rourke. 'There's one more man at least in the house, but we'll see what little Mister Pelton can tell us about all this.'

CHAPTER THIRTY-TWO

More Game

Mr. Pelton had taken command of himself again with a deal of rapidity. He was brushing from his clothes assiduously the dust of the side-walk where he had fallen when O'Rourke's bulldog grip was upon him. He was neatly turned out in a blue suit and black shoes and a blue tie spotted with fine points of gold. A blue-trimmed handkerchief peeped appropriately from the breast pocket of his coat. The police no longer kept their hands on him, and he had fallen into an attitude of easy grace such as the well dressed are apt to adopt, seeming to fit themselves better to their clothes with every move that they make.

'Now break right out and tell us what happened,' demanded O'Rourke.

'I'll search the top of the house with my men,' said the sergeant. 'You two can take care of this fellow, I guess?'

'You'll stay down here with us, if you don't mind,' suggested Campbell. 'When we start to search the upstairs of this place, we'll go two by two and try to act like mice. We don't want to go rolling through the place like a herd of

234

bulls, Sergeant, if you don't mind.'

'By the way of them talking,' said the sergeant, who was a good natured man after all, 'you'd think that we had no brains at all here in Chicago . . . But go on, man, and get to the meat of the thing.'

'It will have to come out in a court of law, I know,' said Pelton. 'I'd rather keep it for that time, Mister O'Rourke, if you don't mind.'

'I don't mind at all,' said O'Rourke. 'But if a man's caught with the blood practically dripping off his hands, mostly it's a good idea for him to tell the folks how innocent he is on the spot. Afterwards it sounds like the lawyer might've given some advice.'

'I think you're right,' Pelton agreed with extraordinary coolness. He touched the tape on his upper lip and frowned a little, as though the lip pained him when he spoke; then he went on: 'The fact is that Grosvenor is a blackmailer.'

'So you followed him up and slipped a knife into him?' nodded O'Rourke pleasantly.

Pelton listened to the interruption with perfect calm and, when it was ended, he went on.

'There's a matter of a woman in the business, and I'll leave her name out until the court wants it from me. Is that all right?' he asked.

'It's all right,' said O'Rourke. 'Ten years after they set the whole world on fire, there's

235

mighty few women that're worth remembering the names of. Go ahead.'

'Leave the man talk and stop chattering, Pat,' advised Campbell.

Pelton smiled faint thanks towards the Scotchman. He continued: 'I happened to meet Grosvenor here in Chicago. That is to say, I ran into him on the street. He cornered me at once. The man was broke. He was desperately ugly. He wanted money, or else he threatened to talk about that rotten spot in my past. I'm hoping to be married to a charming girl before long, Mister O'Rourke, and the sort of filth that Grosvenor would have built up with lies out of a very ordinary peccadillo would have smashed everything. I went out and got the money for Mister Grosvenor, therefore. I paid him five thousand dollars.'

'Correct,' said O'Rourke.

'But I wasn't content with that,' continued Pelton. 'The fact is that the fear of blackmail was chilling my soul. I wondered what could be done about such a beast as Grosvenor. So I thought it might be a possibility for me to call in the police and have them watch him. He's a fellow with an unsavory reputation. If he were pointed out, I thought that the law might do something constructive to put him under cover.'

'That's a reasonable kind of an idea,' said the sergeant.

'The fact is that I followed him,' said Pelton,

'when he left the Clifton. And before long I saw that *he* was following another man. That man was you, Mister Campbell.'

'Was it?' said Campbell. 'Couldn't you have hooted a warning to me, then?'

'When you went down the block and disappeared into the dark for a time,' said Pelton, paying no heed to the interruption, 'Grosvenor hid also, and I got down beside a flight of front steps. I saw you cross the street and enter this house. I saw Grosvenor steal in immediately after you. By that time, frankly, I was very curious. I wondered what a detective and such a fellow as Grosvenor would want to do with one another . . .'

'How did you know that I was Campbell?'

'Grosvenor had told me a little about you. I tiptoed into the cellar here. I was a bit on edge and frightened. I got into the mouth of the hallway. I thought I heard somebody running lightly . . . on tiptoes, so to speak. Then a door closed. Whether on this floor or upstairs I couldn't say. But just as I entered the mouth of that corridor, where the light was very dim, I saw the dead man stretched on the floor. That was too much for me. I turned and ran for my life. You know the rest of this, Mister Campbell.'

'You ran very light on your feet for a fellow that was scared to death,' O'Rourke commented.

'I suppose I did,' said the calm Pelton.

'When you've seen murder, I suppose it puts wings in the heels of most of us. It's the first time that I've seen death . . . like that.'

He closed his eyes and shuddered. It was only a single spasm.

'You've told the whole truth about this?' asked Campbell.

Pelton looked straight at him.

'No,' he said at last. 'I've left out one part that makes things a good deal blacker for me. The fact is that Grosvenor had written me a threatening letter and commanded me to meet him with money in Chicago. I was weak enough to telegraph to his train that I would be in Chicago with money for him. No, it was not a chance meeting in the street.'

He drew a long breath and dusted his slender fingers together.

'Well, I'm glad that I've told the whole story out,' he said.

'It sounds straight,' said O'Rourke. 'You've got kind of the black look of that John Cobb about you but, aside from that, I guess you're a straight fellow, Pelton.'

Pelton accepted the compliment with the faintest of smiles.

'We'll just keep a good watch on him though,' said Campbell.

'I expect that, of course,' said Pelton.

'There's no reason to expect it,' answered O'Rourke, 'but the way of it is that, Angus is a Scotchman, and he wouldn't leave a penny of advantage out of his hand.'

'It's very natural and very right,' said Pelton. 'I hope that I can be bailed out soon, however. I am bound for the funeral of my closest relative, Mister Campbell.'

'Did you like him?' asked Campbell curiously. 'Was he a fellow that meant a lot to you outside of hard cash?'

Pelton looked down. The eye of Campbell burned at him.

'He was very close,' said Pelton in a soft voice.

'Well . . .?' said the sergeant.

At this moment they heard, distinctly, a murmuring of feet along the floor above them. The sounds moved toward the back of the house.

'They may be coming down . . . there's more than Latimer,' muttered O'Rourke. 'Sergeant . . . Harry . . . all of you, get back inside the doors of these rooms along the hall. Heave Grosvenor out of the way. Out every light. When I signal you, maybe we'll have something to see.'

Campbell merely said: 'My job is you, Pelton. Stay close to me. I'll have a gun at the small of your back. No monkeyshines, Pelton.'

'My dear fellow,' said Pelton, 'do you suspect me as much as all this?'

'I dunno,' said Campbell. 'I might have to see you burn in the chair, after all. There's just the chance, and I'm a frugal man, Pelton. I don't waste the chances when I find them.'

'Right you are,' said Pelton.

O'Rourke's whispering instructions had set the police at work, and their rubber-heeled shoes made little noise on the floor as they lifted the body of Grosvenor, his long arms dipping down as they carried him into the nearest room. All in a trice that narrow little corridor was empty except for some glistening spots of blood which lay where Grosvenor had died.

The last flashlight had gone out before O'Rourke heard the sound of a door opening distinctly, above them and at the back of the cellar. At the same time a thin whistling of wind ran through the room.

After that quiet footfalls descended. Someone stumbled and cursed under breath. Then the wavering brilliance of a torchlight went flaming down the cellar corridor. An automobile went by in the street and honked like a wild goose at the next corner.

The voice of a man muttered something.

'Now,' said O'Rourke quite loudly and shone the torch from his hand straight towards the people in the corridor.

It was Pete he saw first and half a step behind him chunky Champion, already with a gun half out of his clothes.

O'Rourke said: 'Don't run, boys.'

The police torches were flashing before this. They sidestepped through the doorways, their guns ready, a grim lot. For it takes a grim fellow to do Chicago police work. Grimness is in their legend, one might say.

'We won't run,' said Pete with his usual coolness. 'Hello, Mister O'Rourke. It's off again, on again, Finnegan, ain't it, between you and me?'

'You're on again, Pete,' said O'Rourke. 'And you're going to stay on till you burn. Boys, get some handcuffs on these two thugs, will you? Iron 'em each separate, and then once together, and one of you for an anchor, eh?'

'They look a kind of harmless old pair,' said the sergeant.

'Do they?' answered O'Rourke. 'I'll tell you what they are . . . they're the heat that comes out of the flame, and the bang that comes out of the lightning, and the blood that follows a knife. There's nobody like 'em. You have 'em in your hands one minute, and then they're gone. They've made a fool of me. Now I'll make a choppin' block out of *them*!'

'Speak soft,' said Campbell. 'You are letting your voice out, Pat, and there's still Latimer over our heads. You still got a pair of handcuffs, brother? I can use it on this fellow here . . . this Gentleman Jim Pelton.'

'Handcuffs?' murmured Pelton, and then he laughed a little, and made the laughter stop as though he were a little ashamed of being amused by such grave men.

'Now back for the stairs,' said O'Rourke.

241

'Every man with feathers between his toes. Mind the steps don't creak when you're climbing, and we'll gather Latimer in, bless him, and have the crowd of them cooped, except the girl.'

He already had started for the back stairs when the voice of Champion rolled in a tremendous thunder through the cellar: 'Charlie! Police! Charlie!'

CHAPTER THIRTY-THREE

Getaway

The thick and booming uproar of Champion's voice came loudly enough but with all the syllables obscured through the floor to big Latimer. Yet he made the meaning clearly enough, and the warning lifted him as with wings out of his chair and into the hall of the first floor. At the same time a thunder of footfalls fell upon the back stairs.

He leaped for the front door. The grim outline of the police car standing at the curb waited for him there. He could, in fact, have flung the door open and raced safely down the front way, but he could not know that. So he turned and sprinted for the stairs with a graceful dignity from the first floor to the upper regions of the house, the great well diminishing as the stairway circled twice around, above. Three at a time he took the steps and reached the second floor as the uproar poured into the hallway beneath.

Outside the house a siren began to sound, and his heart floated up into his throat, buoyed by the shrilling cry. He turned onto the last flight of the circling stairs. It was then that he heard the brief rattling of footfalls, quick, leaping footfalls, above him.

He went on, with a gun in his hand, one eye measuring the treads and one scanning the darkness which his flashlight probed. He had a glimpse of a figure well above, as he gained the top hallway, a form vanishing through the door that led to the unlighted attic stairs.

He gained the door. It was his only chance. If that scout closed the door to the roof, he was hopelessly and helplessly imprisoned in the house. The mere dropping of the latch would see to that. Only the dry, sharp vision of Campbell could have thought of getting some soft-footed forerunner into the upper part of the house to cut off all escape, thought Latimer.

He reached the narrows of the attic stairs. The torch showed him the closed door, and hopelessly he beat his fists against it. It jerked open instantly before him and let him out under the stars, for the night had turned clear, bitterly cold, and bright as a face.

Automatically he dropped the outer bolt which was used in stormy weather. There was a way of prying it up from the inside, but the way took whole minutes.

Now, crouching with his gun, he scanned the sharp slant of the roof and the blunt fists of the chimney pots. Off to the right a form stood, clearly seen against the stippling of the stars. It was no man but a woman! She stood on the very verge of the gutter, balancing for the long leap to the next roof's edge.

'Not there,' he called. He knew her by something indefinably light and graceful. 'Jo, not there! It's too far for you . . . the other side . . .!'

The pursuit boiled up right against the attic upper door and smashed at it with gun butts. And still that siren screamed through the street; and other answering sirens shrilled far off and nearer. The whole armed strength of the city might be pooled there before long.

The girl had turned and made a single pace back up the slant of the roof. He himself hardly dared to stand but scrambled on all fours to the ridge. She, however, ran lightly up after him. She stood there again, secure as a tightrope walker, while the wind set her teetering.

'Charles, go on . . . I'll care for myself.'

He thought he heard her say that, but the damned wind was blowing a numbness through his brain, and dimming his eyes, and putting a

244

weird voice at his ear. Down the opposite, sharp slope of the roof he clambered, tearing off his shoes on the way. He stood on the verge, hooking his toes over the roof edge. It was not a very easy jump for one standing in such a precarious position. Then a light body ran past him, dark above and pale below ... the girl with her skirts knotted at the waist, wonderfully small in her stockinged feet. Jumping from the run, she cleared the gap lightly before him. He, swinging his arms forward and up with all his might, sprang in turn, balanced horribly on the farther edge, and felt the strong tug of her hand drawing him forward to safety.

A splintering crash from the roof of the old Latimer house ... that was the roof door going down under the gun butts.

Well, let clodhopper policemen try to bridge the gap that he and the girl had flown over. They went swiftly up to the ridge and scrambled over on the other side, Latimer on his hands and knees, and the easy form of the girl running upright as though a misstep would not have hurled her down to the concrete pavement below.

He found what he remembered out of his boyhood when he and the other youngsters in their daredevil period had played all over the roofs and knew them inch by inch, like good Alpine climbers. The door opening into this roof was a flimsy thing, as he recalled it, and so flimsy it turned out to be now, in fact, that a single thrust of his shoulder cracked it from top to bottom. The light from his torch gleamed down the dusty, steep steps beneath.

He was halfway down them when he turned and looked back at the girl. Her knee was at his shoulder. She was leaning out over him, holding to the side rail with one hand and, as the torchlight beat up into her face, she laughed down at Latimer and waved her free hand. Her hair was so tousled that it seemed as though the wind were still blowing through it.

Latimer glanced the flashlight back to the door before him. It was not locked and opened at once upon the uppermost level of the house. Here, also, was the descending well of the stairs. Grasping the banister, he leaned against it for a moment to take wind and thought.

'The front way, Charles,' said the girl. 'They're watching the backs of the houses too closely. See.'

She stood at the head of the stairs, pointing. Across the big window at the end of the hall he could see the flashlights streaming, crossing and recrossing, as the men posted in the back yards of the houses scanned every inch with their torches.

She was right, of course. There would be no breaking out from the rear. But the front?

Even now a new siren was screeching down

the street before the house!

Their feet thudded rapidly down the three flights of the circling stairs to the first floor. Fast as Latimer ran, she was before him at the long, narrow window that looked from the door's side down the front steps.

He stood behind her. Light came in through the window from a random headlight. He saw his breath blowing on her hair. She was so much smaller than he had thought. Her head was hardly higher than his chin. If it had leaned back, it would have pressed against the curve of his throat. And yet she was . . .

'Listen to me,' said Latimer. 'Are you hearing me?'

She turned her head and looked silently up to him.

'I'm going to open the front door. Then I intend to walk down it side by side with you, slowly. You understand? Get your dress down. Slowness is what does the work here, not speed. Slowly down those steps, as though we didn't care. People see what they expect to see. Fugitives ought to be running at full speed. You understand, Jo?'

'I'll do it,' she said, shaking out her skirt to full length again.

'If they look at our feet, we're gone,' explained Latimer. 'Otherwise . . . why, we're simply curious fools from the neighborhood come to see the fun. That's all. You see that car back there? There's no one in that. I'm

247

going to get into it and try to bolt down the street. But while I'm raising a commotion, you'll be covered by what I'm doing. Just walk calmly on down the block . . . Have you got money?'

'I have,' she said, her head still turned, staring up at him.

'Take a taxi. Get down in the old second-hand district where you'll find places open all night. Change taxis a couple of times on the way. Rig yourself up with a coat and shoes. You hear me?'

'I hear you.'

'So long, Jo. You're as game a little crook as ever lived,' said Latimer. 'I'd tell you to get out of this life you're in, but I know you like it. Good bye. We won't have time for that when we get out there.'

She bowed her head.

'Ah!' muttered Latimer in her ear. 'Do you have to keep up the acting even now? Isn't there an ounce of clean decency in you?'

She lifted her face. She grew taller at the same moment, so that he knew she had risen on her toes.

'Will you listen to me?' she asked.

'You don't have to build me up,' said Latimer. 'I'll do my best for you the way it is.'

He started to draw back, but she caught the edge of his coat—as though her hand could stop him.

'I don't want to build you up. I want to tell

you the truth,' said the girl.

Latimer took her face between his hands. 'Why, if there were truth in you,' he said, 'you'd be worth ten men's living and dying.'

'You won't listen?' she pleaded.

He closed his eyes. The small, sweet music of her voice was entering deeply into him, but he answered: 'No, I won't listen.'

He turned from her, opened the front door, and stepped outside it. She, instantly, was beside him. And they walked down the steps without haste.

As they reached the sidewalk, a huge cop rushed at them, grabbed them each by a shoulder, and shook them violently. The head of Jo flopped back and forth under this punishment.

'You damned young fools!' he was shouting. 'Don't you know that we got a murderer trapped right next door?'

'We thought we'd take a look at the fun,' said Josephine Worth.

'Get the hell out of here!' he shouted and shooed them down the street.

Just to the side, hardly ten steps away, stood O'Rourke himself, brightly watchful. He saw the officer shooing away the pair—and O'Rourke looked the other way!

When Latimer reached the car which he had selected, he stepped into it. The girl walked past, out of sight beyond the shoulder of the car.

She was gone. Here, in an instant, she was snatched away from him to an eternity of time and space. He felt a little breathless. With each draught of air he whiffed a delicate nothing of fragrance. That was her perfume. It seemed to take the cold out of the hard autumn night. It brought back a warm, sweet gust of spring.

The car was not locked. He turned the self-starter. The engine hummed, turned over.

A policeman ran at him from across the street.

'Hey, what's that?' he called. 'Stop that! Get out of that car!'

'O'Rourke! Detective O'Rourke!' shouted Latimer in answer. 'He wants this car to . . .'

'Damn Detective O'Rourke! That's my car . . . That's . . . hey, what the devil is the matter with you?'

For Latimer, meshing the gears in low, suddenly shot that heavy car straight at the officer of the law. He had time to spring backwards with a yell.

'Coming right back,' shouted Latimer and slid into second gear.

Something bounded beside the car. He reached for his gun as Josephine Worth sprang to the running board and suddenly clambered in to sit at his side.

CHAPTER THIRTY-FOUR

Common Ground

There were four police cars in that block when Latimer shot the big machine down the street. He saw O'Rourke run out from the sidewalk, his mouth opening and closing as though he were yelling, though the uproar was so great that not a word could be heard. But the explosions of the gun he held were audible enough. The heavy slugs hammered against the bullet-proof glass above the side door.

Latimer took the girl by the shoulder and thrust her to the floor.

She crouched there, crying up at him: 'It's bullet proofed, Charles. They can't get us. They can't get us!'

She began to laugh and clap her hands like a child as Latimer shot down to the end of the block. The car might be bullet proofed but not against a high-power rifle. Who among the police was apt to have such a weapon? Certain slugs were nipping right through the car, from end to end!

It was impossible to go straight on. The tumult had brought out a whole sea of Negroes from the adjoining neighborhood. They packed the next block from sidewalk to sidewalk, a solid, dark sea, lit with a white foam of grinning teeth and bright eyes.

Latimer turned. But the street to the right was almost equally jammed. He turned on the third light, a maneuverable searchlight mounted on the left running board, and shone it down into the faces. The horn had not been able to split the throng apart. But the blinding flare of that light made them dissolve to right and left. He glanced back as the machine rolled slowly ahead. The throng was spilling back into the space that had just been left empty for him and, into that mass, the first of the police cars was bucking slowly. They could not shoot with such a human background. The headlight of a second police automobile pulled around the corner.

Now that living mass thinned, dissolved. He was able to step on the gas, dodged right around one corner, left around another, then fled down a straightaway. The traffic light turned from green to red. He screeched the siren and leaped the car between the surging heads of the crosswise traffic. Other sirens wailed behind him. They had picked up his trail again.

The girl pushed herself up onto the seat and looked back. She began reporting as he dodged the car around corners.

'They're coming faster. Now maybe we've left them. No, they're coming again. The wake you cut with your siren, Charles, is the still water through which they come after you. You have to cut through the traffic, and they take advantage to the full. We can't keep them off. We've got to leave the car!'

He began to hear sounds like steady backfiring. Bullets clicked once or twice against the back of the car.

'Now they're shooting at the tires,' said the calm, clear voice of the girl. 'They'll get us soon unless we leave the car . . .!'

The car staggered as though it had run through a wall. A rear wheel began to bump heavily. The whole machine lurched crazily.

'That's it,' said the girl. 'They've got a rear tire!'

He saw the frozen green of a park lawn off to the left, under the brown smoke of the naked trees. He swerved into the entrance, lurched the car across the narrow drive with a half-skid turn, and leaped out of the machine.

The girl ran past him with her winged step. He strode half a pace behind her. The ice in the wind that she faced must be running lances of cold through her hatless, coatless body, but she sprinted straight on, swerved along a path, and turned down towards the edge of a lake.

He saw her goal then. It was a narrow pier that ran a short distance out into the water. It was incomplete. No boats were tied to it.

Right out on it they ran, and down the step-like irregularity of the unfinished end. Before them steel piers rose from the water, marking the steps the pierhead would have to travel before it reached the destined end, a dozen yards away. On the lowest steps they crouched, the black of the water just beneath them. There was no stir or lapping of the waves. The lake was frozen still, covered with a thin sheet of ice.

Sirens were cutting the air behind them. Cars stopped. Maneuvering searchlights slid out across the lake, as though the ice made it easier for the light to travel. A machine parked right across the lake and began to sweep the surface with its light.

The stockinged feet of Latimer began to tingle. The cold was eating into him. He picked up the girl and settled her in his lap. He wrapped his arms around her. Somehow, with his hands and arms, he seemed able to cover all her body. Her hair blew into his face, back and forth, back and forth. And she kept smiling, her lips a little parted. When the light had struck over her, dimly from the distance, he saw the flash of her eyes, as though they were drinking up all the radiance. She did not move. She was inert as though she had been hypnotized, as though she slept. One of her arms hung down. He had to lift it and draw it across her breast into the warmth. Only her eyes and her smile were living.

He said: 'There's murder in you. There's no more soul in you than there is in a hunting cat. You belong to another man . . . but I love you.'

He had to bend his head far in to touch her lips. They formed under his kiss. She did not move or speak. Only her eyes traveled over his face. Something tapped steadily against his breast. That was her heartbeat.

After that moment she said quickly: 'Wait here. I have an idea.'

She was out of his arms. Even before she was free from him, the iced wind got into her, and he felt her shuddering. She ran up the broken steps of stone and went back along the pier before he could stop her.

Wonder got hold of him. Then the voice of O'Rourke was booming, a flat echo spatting up from the face of the frozen lake.

'Take the pier and go over it! Hello, there. What's coming out of the dark?'

Latimer understood at last. If she went in to them and betrayed his hiding place, they would give her a lighter sentence. A face like that could smile its way into state's evidence easily, no doubt. She would go free and walk with that winged step of hers over the hearts of other men.

Cautiously he peered up over the top of the stones and saw O'Rourke meeting the girl in the middle of the pier. Searchlights from the police cars focused on the scene. He saw the big policemen behind the detective, their frosted breath streaming back over their shoulders in the wind.

He heard the girl say: 'You've got me,

255

Mister O'Rourke. Rather, the cold has me.'

'You're only one bite out of the loaf,' said O'Rourke, pulling off his overcoat and wrapping it around her. 'Where's Latimer? Back there?'

'Latimer? He's a yellow dog,' said the girl. 'He jumped out of the car just as it swerved into the park. He ran like a deer down that street, yonder, and left me alone!'

Latimer stood up. He was very groggy and not with cold. A sort of drunken music began to throb and drum in his brain, for she had made payment in his behalf. She had put herself like a bribe into the hands of the law so that he could go free!

He stood up, stepped to the top of the pier, and walked slowly towards them, with the yell of O'Rourke striking him in the face.

'It's Latimer! It's Latimer!' he was shouting. 'Get your guns on him. Mind him now, and the devil inside him.'

Latimer went straight up slowly. What happened to him had no meaning. They handcuffed his wrists. They anchored him with manacles to a bulky policeman. He looked only at the girl.

'Did you think you could buy me out by paying down yourself?' he asked her. 'Did you think I'd let you?'

She said nothing. Her face was not in the least altered from its still, clear beauty. There was no deforming stretching of her mouth as she wept, but the tears rolled down from her eyes. It seemed to him strange that they did not freeze against the white of it.

O'Rourke was calling out a question to him.

'Be still, O'Rourke,' he said. And O'Rourke was mysteriously silent.

'It's more than you've done for the rest of 'em,' said Latimer, 'including that handsome bucko in Buffalo.'

'Do you mean Jimmy?' she said. 'Ah, Charlie, Charlie, Charlie, couldn't you see by his face? Couldn't you tell that he was my brother?'

They were jammed into O'Rourke's car, presently, close together. Latimer said: 'What was it that Jim was ashamed to do, when you were talking to him?'

'He'd come on to Buffalo partly to be in the East near Cobb, nearer than the far West, at least, and partly because there was a chance for him to get work as an engineer up there. He'd dug up a copy of the old *Willoughby Messenger*, and he had a foolish idea that through it we could fight out the case in the courts and show that we had a right to share in the Cobb estate, because Cobb had robbed us. I begged him to stay on in Buffalo with his engineering work and trust everything to me. But I'd done so many strange things, dropping out of sight in New York and all that, that Jim would hardly trust me. I only barely managed to persuade him. He was ashamed to let me go

257

on alone, you see? He really thought that the mention of the gold strike in the newspaper would be a good basis for a lawsuit.'

'What did the telegram mean?' asked Latimer. 'Dick sinking fast strike now'?'

'It was from my Uncle Tom to tell me that my father was very ill and that, if anything was to be done, it had better be hurried. But father has taken a turn for the better now.'

'Be still,' said O'Rourke. 'Will you close up? Or do I have to put you in separate cars?'

CHAPTER THIRTY-FIVE

Shares

O'Rourke took them back to 2118 Beauregard Street where the police had cordoned the ends of the block. He took them back into the basement of the old house. Here two pairs of exhibitions, carefully recovered from the roof of the building by the searching police, were replaced on the freezing feet of the captives.

They had a whole battery of flashlights to illumine the scene, police everywhere as a background and, in the center of the important group of Pete Winslow and Champion, were the girl with Latimer, Campbell, Lawrence Purvis Pelton, and O'Rourke. Campbell was studying with care a little slide of celluloid and the writing on the back of an old envelope.

O'Rourke, therefore, took command.

'I guess we've got 'em all,' he said. 'Grosvenor's been had, and the rest are all here. Come now, Angus. Have you got a patrol wagon out there, Sergeant, or one car big enough to hold all of us, because I'm not going to be parted from any of these beauties. They've got to go all together.'

Campbell said: 'Wait ... will you wait a minute?'

O'Rourke laughed happily.

'What's there to wait for, brother?' he asked. 'There's everything that we want to ask for. We've got the beef and the tomatoes and the potatoes and the onions and the whole damned stew, ain't we?'

Campbell looked up with the dull, open eye of a sleepwalker.

'Cobb never rode on the train!' he said.

O'Rourke winked at the sergeant. 'Be easy,' he said. 'Humor him a little. He had a great-grand-uncle that used to see ghosts and read dreams. The Scotch are a queer lot entirely. All right, Angus. You and me sat with him in the stateroom and witnessed his will ... but if you say so, John Cobb didn't ride in the train.'

He laughed as he ended this speech.

It had no effect on Campbell. The irony brought no glint into his vacant eye.

'Cobb never stepped on the train,' he said. 'While you and me were in that stateroom,

259

John Cobb was sitting in an iron chair with his face melted black by the fire, and his body roasted like burned pork. Cobb was dead those hours before!'

'This is a good one,' said O'Rourke. 'Go ahead and deduce something for the boys, Angus. He's a regular deducer, like Sherlock Holmes and the rest, Sergeant. He's a book detective. Yeah, he reads books and studies things. Takes night courses in ballistics, and the study of handwriting, and he's a fingerprint expert, too. There's nobody like old Angus. So go on and deduce, Angus. Let's hear you.'

'It's the handwriting that does the trick,' said Campbell, his face as lost in a dream as before. 'D'you see, Pat? Here in the will and there in the signature of the real John Cobb at the bottom of his picture are the writing of the dirty hound that murdered John Cobb. He then dressed in his clothes and went to New York for protection, and used us for goats to witness the will he forged for himself, and uncorked the chloroform bottle, and stopped the train, and slid himself out the window, and dragged a trail back to the place where the dead man already was sitting . . .'

'Look out,' called the sergeant.

As a matter of fact there was no need to beware. It was simply that Lawrence P. Pelton had fainted to the floor.

*   *   *

'It couldn't be,' said O'Rourke at the police station, with whiskey before him and a cigar gripped in his teeth. 'You could scare Pelton damned near to death, but it couldn't be true. How could Pelton have wangled getting to Cobb's place then leave the train and back to his home in Minnesota?'

'He had a high-power plane that could do damned near two hundred miles an hour,' said Campbell.

'The plane was broken and useless, man.'

'It was not. That was the alibi. There was only a part missing. A part *missing*. Hell, Pat, couldn't you see how easy that was? He calls out a mechanic and shows him a broken part. Before the mechanic has got back to Lassiter, long before, that plane of Pelton's is hitting it up through the sky. It's not so many thousands of miles. Six or seven hours, eh? Oh, he had plenty of time, if he worked it on a schedule!'

O'Rourke stared like a punch-drunk pugilist.

'He's got an amphibian,' said Campbell. 'He lands it in the Hudson, where it leaves no traces. He goes up to Cobb's house. He takes him for a walk into the woods, and along in the dark of the evening he murders John Cobb. He goes back to the house, dresses in Cobb's clothes, telephones in Cobb's name to Corrigan, gets to the train. He has the look of Cobb about him, small, dark, mustache, and all. But he don't take chances. He keeps his hat down and his collar up. Remember he wouldn't have light in the stateroom? And you and me damning him for a coward and a fool? He forges the will under our noses, with the jerking of the train to explain why the writing's so wobbly. All except the signature. And he has that down pretty pat. He's practiced that a million times, I suppose. He flows it off. A pretty good thing, if nobody looks at it close. But if a man that knows ... if a man that's studied handwriting by night ... if a man like that takes one good look ... he sees that it's master Lawrence Pelton that done the writing!'

O'Rourke, stunned, swallowed his glass of whiskey, and refilled it carefully.

'He wrote the letters that had scared Cobb and made Cobb whine to Corrigan before?' suggested O'Rourke feebly.

'Not him,' said Campbell. 'Those letters came from people that had a reason for knifing Cobb. The people he'd crooked out West at the Willoughby Lode. He writes and tells Pelton he's in fear for his life. He's coming West to get some bigger spaces between him and the horizon. He'll take such and such a train. He reserves a seat on it. When Pelton hears that, he sees his chance. He writes the letter that promises the killing of Cobb before the morning of that day. He frames his alibi by calling the mechanic. Then he comes on the jump. But some of those others from the West ... they've got wind that Cobb is going to move. They make connections with that same train.'

'Angus,' said O'Rourke sadly, 'I been a fool, and you've got the real brain!'

'You found the sand. You found the footprint. You found the dead man,' said Campbell. 'Where would I have been without all that groundwork done?'

'Would you kindly mind tellin' me, Angus,' said O'Rourke, 'what got your head jumping first of all on Pelton?'

'It was thinking how much of a family look there was between this Pelton and Cobb, except that he didn't have a mustache. And then I read that Pelton *did* have a mustache that happened to get burned off. D'you see? Was there ever a man that thought farther back behind everything that he did? He takes off the mustache. Suppose that the witnesses to the will see him afterwards, they won't recognize him as the man that rode in the stateroom with him. It all works out. There's only Grosvenor. He wasn't a part of the seven that were robbed by John Cobb. How does he come into this?'

'On the side, I can see that now,' said O'Rourke. 'Go back to Pelton dressed in the clothes of John Cobb and making for the train. He knows it's unlikely that anybody'll be there that would know John Cobb, that lives so much to himself. It's not likely, neither, that anybody'll be there that knows Pelton from the West. Still there's plenty of people on a big train. And one of them looks at Pelton and knows him sure. D'you see?'

'I *do* see!' cried Campbell. 'Afterwards he comes back to the stateroom and sees Pelton. He wonders is Pelton sick, that he acts so strange. He sits down in that stateroom and talks, and Pelton, ah, man! ... what a sick fellow is Pelton when he knows he's recognized.'

'Aye, it would spoil everything,' said O'Rourke. 'For the case of Pelton all hangs on the point that John Cobb is riding on that train. And that he himself is away back there in Minnesota. It's too late for him to change. Cobb's dead already. The will's forged and in the hands of Campbell. There's only one chance to take ... to put all the cards face up in front of Grosvenor ... knowing him for a dirty dog ... and to offer him fifty per cent of the deal. You see, Angus?'

'Of course I see. It's beautiful, Pat. It's a beautiful thing, ain't it?'

'It is,' said O'Rourke. 'That's why Grosvenor got the five thousand. Just an earnest of what's to come when the estate's settled. But Pelton won't trust him. He don't want that leech suckin' the blood out of him. So he followed Grosvenor out of the hotel.'

'Till the point where he sees Grosvenor on

264

top of me, ready for murder,' broke in Campbell. 'And it means nothing to Pelton except a chance to stab Grosvenor in the back. He's already got a handkerchief of Grosvenor's that he's picked up in his hotel room perhaps. And so he wraps that around his hand and slides the knife into the back of Grosvenor ... and runs right out into the hands of Pat O'Rourke.'

*   *   *

O'Rourke, that same day, said to Peter Winslow: 'Suppose that young McGuire didn't appear to press the charge against you, Pete? Would that open you up and make you talk?'

'Will you do that for me?' asked Winslow.

'I've done it,' said O'Rourke.

'Why, give me a drink, then,' said Pete, 'and I'll tell you the whole yarn.'

He began slowly: 'Go back to the day that me and Jay Markham went prospecting in the name of us and the other five that had formed a kind of a company to split up any luck that any of us found. And that day we *do* find luck. It's back in the sand dunes that a knob of rock sticks six inches out of the sand. We tap it. It cracks open and shows us the dog-gonedest thing that any man ever seen. Why, only the weight of that rock was enough of a story. We shoveled away some of the sand and saw where the vein ran. We shoveled the sand back. We went on along the direction of it. And did you remember the two lines across the map, at the angles, up on top?'

'I remember,' said O'Rourke, nodding.

'That's where we found more outcroppings. And we come back to the dot ... that was where we'd started from that day and where we'd been digging. We mapped every foot of the way, and then Markham says to me that we ought to keep this under our hats, because likely there's millions in it, and so we shouldn't say a word to the other five.

'That made me sour. I damned him for the idea, and a minute later he tried to hit me with his pick, and I shot him. I went back into camp with our specimen, and you know the rest. Even the five of them that I'd held out for doubted me, except good old Alec Latimer. So I went up for life. But I made up my mind that nobody'd get rich on what I'd found, and I hid the map before I went to prison. I'll cut through all those years to the time when I met up with John Cobb. He was wearing a different name, and he was in for a year for some dirty job. But I sort of liked him. One day I told him the yarn. He went wild. He told me when he got out he'd work the locations if I'd give 'em to him, and then he'd buy me out of the prison.

'Of course an old hand like me only laughed at him. He asked if he could buy me out, would I give him the half share? I said I would, of course, and thought no more about it. He's not free for six months before I get my pardon and walk out. Where Cobb got the money, I don't know. More dirty work, I suppose. Anyway, there I was free, and I led Cobb right to the place where the plan was located. It was the last that I ever saw of the map. He kept promising to show it to me. And in the meantime he locates and starts work on those two upper points. It's thirty years, nearly, since I've looked at the map, and the distances I've all forgotten. And who could find anything in that rolling sea of sand except he had a map to go by?

'Well, there was machinery and things to buy, and Cobb ran everything. When I asked him what he was making, he said that it was slow pay, and that the machinery was eating up a lot of the profits, but just the same he was giving me plenty of money, a thousand every ten days or so. And I didn't think too much till he'd cleaned out the two veins in short order, and suddenly he folds up and goes back East. He'd taken out millions, d'you see? When I heard how rich he was, I tried to get close to him. It was no good. He kept me off, and I didn't have a legal claim in the world.

'All I knew was that the first strike me and Markham had made, the richest of all, hadn't been worked. Cobb's idea, I guess, was to wait until things settled down and then go out and clean that up, too. The trouble he wanted to settle down was because I'd turned to the old members of the seven partners. I told 'em everything ... how Cobb was robbing me and that meant them, too. I got them together. Markham was dead, of course. So was Latimer, the best of the lot. But Alex Latimer had left a son able to fill his shoes, as maybe you know, O'Rourke. Dick Worth was sick and left only a girl, his niece, to carry on for him. Glenn and Waterson, both dead without heirs.

'There was left old Harry Champion and Josephine Worth and Charlie Latimer and me. You see? I break the news to them all, and we plan things together ... the three men, mostly, because the girl's only a girl, and we leave her pretty much out. Latimer never even laid eyes on her till he chanced into her on the train, don't you see?

'We begin to put the pressure on Cobb. Champ writes the letters with my help. Latimer goes out East to keep an eye on Cobb. We put on pressure, and it's plain that Cobb is scared. We all gather in New York, with Latimer putting up the cash for us. And now there's where a big chance comes in. Because out from the West they send Josephine Worth. Her uncle is dead sick, and they want to get something out of Mister Robber Cobb. She comes on, tries to see Cobb, gets shut out of the house, and finally tails him to the train just the way Latimer tails him to the train.

'Because Latimer had cut in on Cobb enough to know that that reservation on the train had been made. He calls me and Champ out to the country to try to search the house for the map while he tails Cobb to Chicago and sees what's happening out there. You know most of the rest of it. On the train Jo goes and pleads with the man she thinks is Cobb. He throws her out.

'Latimer gets in there for a minute, too, but Pelton won't let him stay, and he don't recognize the difference between Pelton and the real Cobb in the half light. All he does, like a mug, is to think that Jo Worth is a crook, and he starts following her crookedness ... and then you are on the spot and ready to raise hell ... and a whole lot of trouble nearly got started, Mister O'Rourke.'

*   *   *

'And what,' said Campbell one day, as he sat with Latimer and Mrs. Charles (Josephine) Latimer, 'was the reason that Cobb would have all those pictures hanging in that dressing room? What would he want of those?'

'Because he lived on meanness the way a cat lives on milk, Campbell,' said Latimer. 'Every day, out in the quiet of that house of his, when he dressed, or when he undressed, he thought about how he had trimmed seven men, living or dead. He had the pictures of some of the dead men. He put mine into the group to represent my dead father. I suppose it was a thing that made him laugh twice a day.'

'His money goes all to the state. There's not one of you that can put a claim in for it, is there?' asked Campbell.

'Not a one,' said Latimer. 'We've lost that. But there's still the richest vein of all to work. The company of Worth, Latimer, Champion, and Winslow are going to work it. We're thinking of putting down some shares in the names of Campbell and O'Rourke.'

'It's a good thought,' said Campbell. 'But will you tell me one thing, Jo? Tell me the truth about the poor devil of a fellow at headquarters who has confessed that as soon as the man from Cobb's house telephoned in, he phoned back to you to tell you that Cobb was taking the train. Is that the truth?'

'When I got to New York,' she said, 'I was hungry to see John Cobb and beg him to do right by my father. We thought that Dad was dying just then. And to keep track of him and where he might dodge to, I saw one of the men that sat at the telephone exchange in police . . . I'm sorry if I've hurt his career as a policeman.'

'You didn't hurt him,' said Campbell. 'The dog was a regular leak that passed out news about more cases than yours . . .! Did you think, really, that talking to John Cobb would do your case any good?'

'I did hope so,' she said.

Campbell and Latimer looked steadily at

one another, smiling with the superior wisdom, the pitying super knowledge, of the stronger sex. The girl, watching them, would not let herself smile at all. There was only a faint light of mockery in her eyes.

We hope you have enjoyed this Large Print book. Other Chivers Press or G.K. Hall & Co. Large Print books are available at your library or directly from the publishers.

For more information about current and forthcoming titles, please call or write, without obligation, to:

Chivers Press Limited
Windsor Bridge Road
Bath BA2 3AX
England
Tel. (01225) 335336

OR

G.K. Hall & Co.
P.O. Box 159
Thorndike, Maine 04986
USA
Tel. (800) 223-2336

All our Large Print titles are designed for easy reading, and all our books are made to last.